T0165553

Arabian War Games

Arabian War Games

Cataclysmic Wars Redraw the
Map of the Middle East

Ali Shihabi

ARABIAN WAR GAMES
CATACLYSMIC WARS REDRAW THE
MAP OF THE MIDDLE EAST

iUniverse books may be ordered through booksellers or by contacting:

iUniverse
1663 Liberty Drive
Bloomington, IN 47403
www.iuniverse.com
1-800-Authors (1-800-288-4677)

ISBN: 978-1-4697-8486-1 (sc)
ISBN: 978-1-4697-8487-8 (hc)
ISBN: 978-1-4697-8488-5 (e)

Library of Congress Control Number: 2012903438

Print information available on the last page.

iUniverse rev. date: 11/12/2019

Acknowledgments

I would like to thank my editor Sandy Brown for her hard work, dedication, and patience with my endless edits. Her suggestions and corrections have added much to the quality of this book. I would also like to thank Daniel Slone, my military affairs editor and consultant, whose practical knowledge and on-the-ground experience in the region was essential in ensuring that the military scenarios set out in this book are realistic. I am also particularly grateful to my darling wife, Nadia, for her support, encouragement, and invaluable input throughout this project. To her I dedicate this book.

Contents

Persian/Arabian Gulf Region

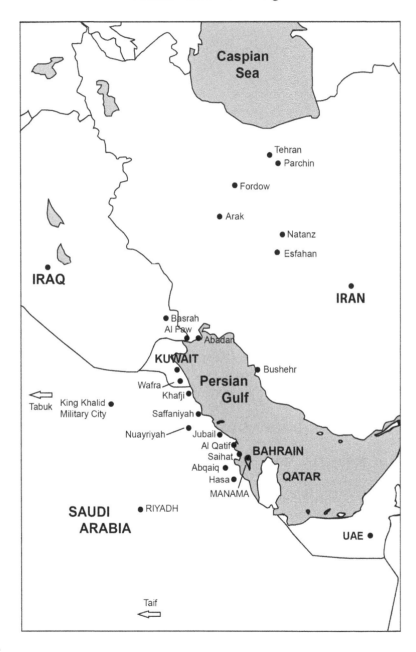

Israel/Palestine Region

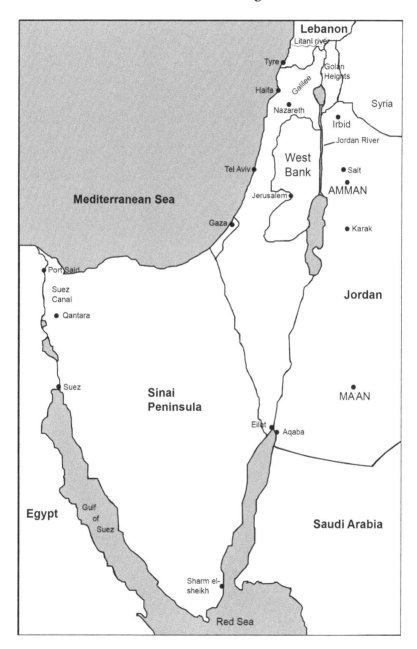

Preface

The political fuel that is propelling societies to war over the next few years should be clearly discernible today.1

—Professor Colin Gray, Centre for Strategic Studies, University of Reading

This is a future history, a fictional work that makes political and military predictions. It takes growing Arabian-Iranian tensions and the long-festering Palestinian-Israeli conflict and extrapolates these into a possible future conflict scenario.

As Nassim Taleb explains in his book *The Black Swan*,[2] man is demonstrably arrogant about what he thinks he knows, and hence he underestimates uncertainty by compressing the range of possible future outcomes. Not only do we lack imagination about the future, Taleb points out, but also we repress others' imagination of the future. This can be clearly seen in the tendency of professional predictors to avoid forecasting anything "outlandish," even though human experience should

---

[1] Colin S. Gray, *Another Bloody Century: Future Warfare* (London: Weidenfeld and Nicolson, 2005), 21.

[2] Nassim Nicholas Taleb, *The Black Swan: The Impact of the Highly Improbable* (New York: Random House, 2007).

have taught us that *history does not crawl but in fact jumps between significant shocks.*

To wit, both Israel as a "Jewish state" and Iran as the "Islamic Republic" face emerging existential threats to their survival, *as they see it*, which they may find virtually impossible to address without provoking war. In Israel, the "Jewish state" is slowly sinking in an ocean of millions of Palestinians, both in Israel itself and in the surrounding territories—a problem that, despite all the peace talk, many of Israel's increasingly right-wing elites believe can only be "solved" through the use of force. At the same time, Iran is slowly choking on heavy sanctions amid a widespread regional perception of weakening American deterrence and could therefore become more emboldened to risk invading eastern Arabia[3] in what would be a desperate attempt to avoid economic ruin and possible regime change.

The "outlandish" scenarios I present in *Arabian War Games* will, I hope, provoke some critically needed *creative thinking* about these most dangerous issues facing the region today.

---

[3] "Arabia" and "Arabian" are used here to designate the countries located in the Arabian Peninsula—Saudi Arabia, Kuwait, Bahrain, Qatar, the United Arab Emirates (UAE), and Oman—that constitute the Gulf Cooperation Council (GCC). A wider definition of "Arabia" can include Yemen and also encompass the tribal lands of southern Jordan and Iraq.

Chapter 1: Operation Imam Hussein

Keep scratching and what you find at the bottom of Iran's soul is a newfound taste for empire.[4]

—Former CIA official Robert Baer

The Shia, a dissident breakaway faction of Islam, have historically felt discriminated against in Sunni-majority countries. The 1979 Iranian Revolution led by Shia theocrats inspired many Shia,[5] who saw in it a potential force that could support them against their Sunni overlords. Iran's new and ambitious revolutionary leaders, in turn, recognized the opportunity that this Shia affinity presented them with, which was to drive a wedge into Arabia and spread their "revolution" into the heartland of oil and of Islam.

---

[4] Robert Baer, *The Devil We Know: Dealing with the New Iranian Superpower* (New York: Crown, 2008), 4.

[5] Arab Shia are spread around the Gulf in the following population concentrations (defining the exact percentage in each Arab country is a politically charged/disputed issue):

Bahrain—majority Shia
Iraq—majority Shia
Kuwait—10 percent to 30 percent Shia
Saudi Arabia—10 percent Shia

This ambition quickly provoked a decade-long war, begun in 1980, between Iran and Saddam Hussein's then Sunni-minority-led Iraq. That war ultimately weakened Iran and frustrated its leaders' early attempts to penetrate Arabia. The Iraqi barrier against Iranian expansionism broke down, however, in 2003, when the United States invaded Iraq, overthrew Saddam, and allowed a Shia-dominated regime to take over. Iran, hardly believing its luck, quickly began building its influence in the new Iraq.

Attempting to become a regional hegemon, however, is a very costly business, and the accumulated political and economic price of Iran's obsession to dominate the region has now become overwhelming.

Iran's oil production, its economic lifeblood, is today only 20 percent of what it was before the 1979 revolution, while the Iranian population has more than doubled since that time. The long war with Iraq destroyed critical infrastructure, particularly in the oil sector, which has never been adequately rebuilt. That war also introduced a culture of perpetual subsidies, which the regime constantly has to tip up in order to bribe the masses into submission. These subsidies, while very costly to maintain, are ever so dangerous to tamper with. In fact, the Iranian government's attempts to reduce them unleash wide popular outrage. Added to these economic challenges are Iran's substantial ongoing costs of supporting its foreign clients such as Hezbollah, as well as its massive military expenditures, including a very expensive nuclear weapons and ballistic missile program.

As if that were not enough, all of this has been occurring under the shadow of onerous economic sanctions imposed by the United States and its allies, sanctions that have become even tighter in recent years as the Iranian nuclear weapons program nears fruition. These actions are choking the Iranian economy of goods, services, and trade and are barring Iran's access to the global financial system. Another ramification of the sanctions has been the emergence of multiple avenues of corruption and patronage that make Iran's economy even more dysfunctional and its leadership ever-increasingly unpopular. And now the ultimate embarrassment for the mullahs is that Iran, a major oil producer, is running out of gasoline. Its crumbling oil refineries are unable to meet local demand, with sanctions on the import of gasoline into the country compounding the problem.

All of these factors, combined with a collapse of the currency, runaway inflation, high unemployment, and negative growth, are bringing the economy to a virtual standstill, provoking massive social unrest and domestic political turmoil as Iranians angrily question why their limited resources are spent abroad on projecting military power and not at home for basic needs and development.

It is nearly autumn of 20XX, and the lights are about to go out across the Islamic Republic.

Supreme Leader Ayatollah Ali Motahidi is a troubled man. It is only recently that he became leader, in the footsteps of the revered Ayatollah Khomeini and his successor. Following in the footsteps of the leaders of the revolution and the founder of the Islamic Republic always promised to be difficult, and Motahidi continually worries that his people and history alike will perceive him as having failed to preserve and consolidate what he inherited from his mentors. While he has personally succeeded in securing a virtual omnipotence over the different factions of the regime, he realizes that now the Islamic Republic is fighting for its very survival.

Motahidi, supreme commander of the armed forces, has reached the painful conclusion that the only card he has left to play in saving his regime is to use Iran's military strength, fortified by a battle-hardened and ideologically indoctrinated million-man army, to take full control of the Persian Gulf, grab control of Arab oil, and make his country rich and powerful again as the regional hegemon. Iran, he ponders, with its nearly eighty-three million people, the heir to a glorious civilization and the birthplace of the modern Islamic Revolution, cannot allow itself to be slowly strangled to death by these infidels and their Arab poodles.

The Islamic Republic is strong in faith, determination, and its ability to absorb extreme punishment, he reminds himself. *We look not only to this world but also, and more importantly, to the next, eternal world, while the infidel and his Arab lackeys are obsessed with only the present. We will fight and fight hard, willingly sacrificing hundreds of thousands of casualties for our ultimate glory. The Americans, however, lose a few boys and then, like women, melt into a collective emotional breakdown. They have no stomach for the long war. That is our real strength, and we need to use it. Until now, we have allowed the Americans and the Zionists to set the rules of the game. I will change that to make sure that the game is played in the sport we, not they, are best at: that of total war, a war of human endurance, suffering, and sacrifice, not the high-technology video-game war at which the Americans excel. We will set the rules of play, not they, and then God will grant us ultimate victory.*

Tehran, Iran
2 p.m., Friday, September 9

It is a brisk late summer day when the supreme leader summons and subsequently receives in audience the team he has tasked with finalizing preparations for Operation Imam Hussein, the master plan to take Arabia, its oil fields, and eventually its holy cities from its current rulers, the Al Saud and their fellow oil sheikhs.

The meeting is to take place inside Motahidi's drab and austere quarters, a windowless and sparsely furnished room with a huge portrait of Ayatollah Khomeini and the green, white, and red flag of Iran—redesigned in 1980 to reflect changes brought about by the revolution—as the only decorations. Tea has been prepared for them; a full tray sits atop a very low stool in the center of the room. A southerly wind off the Caspian Sea mixing with humidity trapped by the Alborz Mountains north of Tehran has made today chillier than usual for early September. The arriving men are all grateful for the warming refreshment, serving themselves from the kettle and then taking their places on the floor. The supreme leader sits in a walnut armchair while the group faces him cross-legged on the carpet, a scene reminiscent of an imam with his students. By combining the spiritual and temporal authority in one person, the regime has created a halo of quasi divinity around the supreme leader, of which he cleverly takes full advantage in controlling this large and somewhat unruly elite group of the Islamic Republic with its myriad factions, sects, parties, and occasionally even dissident groups.

Those present include National Security Advisor Saeed Jalili, Defense Minister Amir Rowhani, and General Javad Zarif, head of the Quds Force, the elite foreign operations unit of the increasingly powerful Islamic Revolutionary Guard Corps. This force is the "Praetorian Guard" of the regime, a position it has used to successfully spread its tentacles into all aspects of political, economic, and security affairs of the republic. Also present is Professor Vali Moslehi, the Iranian American academic who is a close advisor to the supreme leader and who is at the same time surprisingly well-connected in Washington.

The leader also invited Ali Khatami to this meeting—a strange choice given that this man is hardly his close ally or subordinate. Khatami is an ex-president, former speaker of parliament, and master manipulator who now holds the nominal position of chairman of the Assembly of Experts. The designation, however, does his chameleonlike personality little justice. A senior cleric with the rank of *hojatoleslam*, and formerly an aide of the late supreme leader, he had been a key player in facilitating Motahidi's appointment as supreme leader upon his predecessor's death, hoping at that time to be able to manipulate Motahidi, then a relatively junior cleric whom he helped catapult to the supreme leadership over many more senior and eligible candidates for the post. Khatami, however, had underestimated Motahidi's political skills, and the man has proven to be more than his match since taking power, during which time Motahidi consolidated his own power and sidetracked Khatami. This led to Khatami's occasionally playing at being a member of the opposition, but he was careful never to cross the redline and totally burn his bridges with Motahidi. At the same time, Motahidi always kept a close eye on this slippery, sly opponent and made sure he did not stray too far from the party line.

Motahidi had asked Khatami, whose nearly all-white hair, bright white turban, and crisp tab-collar white shirt drain him of color, making him appear pale and cold, to attend this crucial meeting because he wanted him in the tent, rather than outside it, so as to implicate him in the consequences of this massive undertaking. A tricky situation, but it shows Motahidi at his best as a shrewd political player. Khatami, in any event, could hardly turn down the leader's invitation, and his ego could not resist the opportunity to be privy to and part of the planning for such a potentially historic move.

At the same time, Khatami is a very practical theologian. A descendant of a family of rich pistachio merchants, he had made sure his family's commercial holdings adequately prospered during the Islamic Revolution, and hence he and his sons had accumulated considerable assets, relationships, and interests all over the globe. Unlike some of his more spiritual colleagues, he did not believe in sacrificing the present for the afterlife, thank you very much. He enjoyed life and its privileges fully and wanted to make damned sure that his family's interests and wealth were protected. This point was not lost on his more ideologically and spiritually "pure" colleagues in the leadership, and it added to their regarding him with ongoing suspicion.

Motahidi had also wanted to drive home a point with Khatami by including him, which was that Khatami was too senior a member of the revolution to think that he had any hope of a safe exit if the regime collapsed. "If we go," he had told Khatami in private, "they will string you up as quickly as they will any of us. Don't kid yourself, you will hardly be able to rebrand and repackage yourself as a reformer and democrat. You are in it with us up to your neck; you should have no illusions about that." Khatami reluctantly had to agree with that logic. However much he would have liked circumstances to be otherwise, he clearly recognized that he could not escape his association with this regime, and hence they would all sink or swim together.

"Gentlemen," the leader begins by addressing them, "you all realize we are today facing economic collapse as a result of the sanctions instigated by America and supported by her dogs, the Arab sheikhs. Our beloved Islamic Republic, handed to us in trust by Imam Khomeini, will be destroyed if we sit by meekly and accept this fate. Such timidity and weakness, however, is obviously not what the Almighty expects of us. We, the heirs of the great Persian empires of Cyrus and Darius, the descendants of Imam Hussein,[6] peace be upon him, and the rightful leaders of Islam, have no intention of becoming the Bangladesh of the Persian Gulf. We will not allow the corrupt Arab sheikhs, put in

---

[6] The Shia "saint." He was murdered fourteen hundred years ago, an event that is annually commemorated by the Shia on Ashura, their most important and emotional religious day.

power by the British and kept there by the Americans, to wallow in wealth and debauchery, conspiring with the crusaders and Zionists to destroy us. We have to act, and we have to act now." He then turns to Saeed Jalili and invites him to elaborate.

Jalili, like many of Iran's current rulers, attained his position after a career in the elite Revolutionary Guard. A veteran of the Iraq-Iran War, he is a member of a Revolutionary Guard fraternity that is taking control of the country at all levels. A fighter, he has a deep sense of mission and maintains strong faith in the superiority of the Islamic Republic's revolutionary ideology and its natural right to lead the region, a belief that is only strengthened by his unwavering conviction that the Persian is superior to the Arab. Jalili today is one of the most powerful men in the republic. He is also a member of the establishment's messianic fringe, which believes in the return of the Mahdi,[7] a fact he does not actively advertise since it is privately ridiculed by many of the more pragmatic members of the ruling class. The messianic group he is part of believes that the Mahdi will appear on Judgment Day to herald a great new age, and his return will be prompted by a global battle between good and evil, with Iran in the role of good, obviously, and the "great Satan America" and its lackeys, the Arabs, united in the role of evil. Jalili sees his personal purpose in this conflict as fomenter of the ultimate battle, and it is in this capacity that he will achieve ultimate glory.

Jalili, in his late fifties, is also a great believer in the recently articulated concept of "Iranian Islam," which is the Shia faith practiced in Iran as the "true" Islam, and in the urgency to strive for its supremacy over the Sunni faith, particularly in Arabia, the birthplace of Islam. Should that mission succeed, the rest of the Islamic world would follow into Iranian Islam. The ultimate control of Mecca and Medina, Islam's two holy cities, is within

---

[7] The Shia messiah.

Iran's grasp, he believes, and may very well be attained in his lifetime. After all, the Shia Fatimid Empire had controlled these holy cities in the Middle Ages, so why couldn't it happen again, particularly given the opportunity presented by the American withdrawal from the Gulf? In this, the supreme leader and the rest of the leadership wholeheartedly support Jalili's convictions. For them, that is the ultimate goal, a goal so sweet and enticing that they would sacrifice anything to attain it.

"We need to subjugate the Arabs," Jalili begins, resettling the wire-frame spectacles against his temples, "and retake the whole Persian Gulf and its oil; ultimately wrest control of Mecca and Medina; and take over the leadership of Islam. Today, the Almighty is giving us a chance to prove that we are worthy of this honor. We are opposed by a collection of weak Arab states hiding behind America's skirt. They are ripe for us to swallow now that America is fatigued by war, as Professor Moslehi will soon elaborate on, and we are also greatly aided by a dramatic increase in Sunni-Shiite tensions. The Shia takeover of Iraq scared the life out of the Arab Sunnis since they see a resurgent Shia Iraq backed by Iran as striving to overturn hundreds of years of their rule, dominance, and privilege. They have reacted by increasing the persecution of their Shia, who in the end have nobody to turn to but Iran, even if many, if not most, Arab Shia are becoming increasingly wary of us as Persians wanting to dominate them. Ultimately we still have an ideological hard core of Arab Shia who can influence and manipulate elements among the underprivileged elements of the Shia of Arabia into believing that Iran will take care of them. This fissure among the Arabs is one we intend to take full advantage of by invading Arabia under the guise of protecting its Shia from Sunni oppression."

The leader interjects. "Gentlemen, let us here not forget also our historic obligation to exact revenge on the Wahhabi Al Saud of Saudi Arabia, the ultimate custodians of hatred for the Shia faith and its adherents. Remember that it was these Wahhabis who, in 1803, attacked our holy cities of Najaf and Karbala and burned them to the ground. They even destroyed the shrine of our Imam Hussein. This was their first priority, even before going on to occupy Mecca and Medina, so passionate was their hatred of the Shia. Their descendants, the current Al Saud regime, may have forgotten the event by now, but we the Shia never forget, and we carry that burden of vengeance and retribution until the end of time. Also, the Al Saud are the remaining obstacle to our regional supremacy. They are the dominant power among the Gulf Arabs, and they stand in the way of our leading the Muslim world, so we must destroy them, eradicate them and their clergy from the face of this earth, if we are to emerge victorious." Motahidi sits back, finished with this segment of his opening remarks, and sips from his glass cup of tea.

"So," the leader continues, "the time has come for us to rise up in a holy jihad and fulfill our destiny to lead this region and Islam. Imam Hussein is looking down upon us. He has waited fourteen hundred years for men of our caliber who have the ability to take revenge on his killers' descendants and reclaim the leadership of Islam from the Sunni Arab usurpers. Fourteen hundred years of pain and humiliation, for the Shia, will come to an end when we flood the lands of Arabia with the blood of our oppressors and make them pay a thousand times for their arrogance." He then turns to Rowhani. "General, please update us on the progress of our plan."

Rowhani, the defense minister, is also an alumnus of the Revolutionary Guard and an Iraq-Iran War veteran. His appointment had been the final step in the Guard's consolidation of its power across the country, as the Ministry of Defense, with its control over the regular army, navy, and air force, had been the traditional rival of the Guard. Today, however, the army is needed to play a key role in Iran's invasion of Arabia since it has hundreds of thousands of troops at its disposal, which the Guard and the leadership are determined to make use of in feeding a human-wave strategy to overwhelm the Arabs and even the Americans, if necessary. As the Guard's lesser-trained and underequipped sibling, the army is the ideal provider of human fodder for this facet of the operation, and it is Rowhani's job to ensure that it is used to maximum effect in achieving success. The Guard, freed from this less noble but nonetheless crucial enterprise, will then be able to concentrate all its energies on securing strategic, high-value targets.

Rowhani and Jalili are close allies, and while they share a Revolutionary Guard membership background with Javad Zarif, they are not thrilled by the fact that he, as head of the elite Quds Force, has been able to bypass them and establish a direct line to the supreme leader. Zarif, however, with his control of all offshore operations and the tremendous influence he has built for himself in Iraq, is an irreplaceable component of this mission, and they respect that fact. At the same time, all three look with great suspicion upon Professor Moslehi, whom they don't trust given his American nationality, his close US government ties, and his Western affectations and intellectual arrogance.

"Operation Imam Hussein," General Rowhani begins, repositioning his legs beneath himself, his uniform's gold-embroidered mortarboard epaulets rising up as he shifts around, "is a military takeover of Kuwait, eastern Saudi Arabia, and Bahrain as the first step in a plan to ultimately assume control over the whole Arabian Peninsula. Today, historic conditions have afforded us a unique opportunity to carry out such an ambitious plan. With the dissolution of Saddam's Iraq, the Americans not only destroyed our strongest Arab enemy and the main obstacle to our supremacy in the Persian Gulf but also unwittingly gave us an ally and partner in the new Shia-controlled Iraq. Today, the government of Prime Minister al-Mosawi in Iraq is virtually under our control. Our brother General Zarif is the 'shadow ruler' of Iraq, and he maintains militia armies under the guise of the Popular Mobilization Forces (PMF). These forces, trained and officered by our men, are totally reliable to act on our command. The Iraq of today, gentlemen, is a client state, a vassal of the Islamic Republic. *It is also our sword and land bridge into Arabia since it gives us an Arab 'face' to use against our Arab enemies.*

"By mounting a joint Iraqi-Iranian operation, we will surprise, confuse, and overwhelm the Arabs and Americans. Such a partnership between our country and Iraq has never before been plausible, and hence nobody expects it or is prepared for it. The instant message the world will receive when we attack will not be 'Iran invades Arabia' but rather '*Iraq and Iran* invade Arabia,' and that will make a huge difference in America's reaction to this invasion, at least in the critical early days. It will certainly make enough of a difference to delay their decisive response, which will leave open the window of time we need to become embedded in key locations in eastern Arabia. We will come at them, as they themselves would say, from left field." Rowhani strokes his beard contemplatively. While his facial hair resembles Jalili's, the general's hairline is significantly receding, in contrast to the dense tufts on his ally's head.

"For years," he continues, "the Americans and the Arabs have been preparing for naval, missile, and drone attacks originating from our forces in the Persian Gulf. They have focused on what they call our 'asymmetric' skills—our capacity for guerilla warfare and our success in infiltrating Lebanon and Iraq—all the while gaming and training for an attack on their fleet in the Gulf, missile attacks on Arab oil facilities, and our mining the Strait of Hormuz. As a result, they have strengthened the Bahrain-based US Fifth Fleet and built a network of antimissile defenses across the Gulf. What none of them expect, however, and hence for which they are unprepared, is a brazen 'conventional' land invasion into Kuwait from Iraq. The Gulf Arabs and their American masters have not yet understood the depth of hatred that the Iraqi leadership and Shia majority feel toward the oil sheikhs. Hence the opportunity before us today. They cannot imagine that Iraq will now open for us the vulnerable back door to Arabia.

"Here we are confident that we can overwhelm Gulf Arab military capabilities despite massive expenditures. The Arabs realize this, so they still depend on the Americans to deter us. Consequently, our job is to understand how the Americans will react and how best to undermine their will to resist us when the time comes."

"Now that American troops are out of Iraq and Afghanistan," Jalili explains, taking his cue from Rowhani, "the US has little to show for the losses suffered and costs incurred from that whole messy enterprise. America, as a result, is exhibiting all the signs of war fatigue and, because of this, has no desire to become embroiled in another Middle East conflict. Her 'backbone' in the Gulf, basically her determination to uphold the existing order there, has been weakened considerably. America's will to fight in the Gulf today is gone. Only an attack on her troops or civilians will provoke a military response, and we will make absolutely sure we do not touch them unless they attack us first.

"The Americans, after Desert Storm, built a veritable wall of steel along the Kuwaiti-Iraqi border. Since the American occupation of Iraq in 2003, however, the wall was obviously no longer necessary and has gradually been dismantled. Today, America has only a small force in Kuwait. Iraq, after all, is America's new friend and is therefore no longer seen as a threat to Kuwait. Americans want to believe that Iraq is now a 'responsible' player under their influence, and we encourage Prime Minister al-Mosawi to play along with that presumption. So, Iraq's colluding with us in this invasion will shock and confuse the Americans because the same Iraq that will conspire and cooperate with us is the very 'democracy' they created. They are the parents of this Iraqi newborn, and it will take them some time to acknowledge the fact that we have abducted their baby! When they eventually wake up to this embarrassing reality, they may not want to admit it, even to themselves. Embarrassment and denial are powerful human emotions. Who among them wants to concede that after a hundred thousand casualties and trillions of dollars in cost, all America achieved in the end was the handing of Iraq to Iran on a silver platter?"

Jalili then gives Moslehi the floor. Professor Moslehi is a naturalized US citizen, having come from Iran as a student, taken his PhD at Stanford, and stayed on in California building a name and a career for himself as an Iran expert. His books and lectures on Iranian politics are highly regarded, and numerous administrations have sought him out as an advisor. He has also been careful to keep close ties to the regime in Tehran—a necessity, he explains to the Americans with solid logic, so as to stay abreast of developments there and maintain his knowledge base, which they value so highly. At the same time, it happens occasionally that the line between research and advocacy is crossed, and his involvement in Operation Imam Hussein is a clear crossing of that line, something his American masters would certainly not be thrilled to learn about. He is, however, a passionate Iranian nationalist at heart and a strong believer in Iran's natural right to dominate and rule the entire Gulf region and control its valuable hydrocarbon resources. The US, while not aware of the degree of his involvement in higher-level policy making in Iran, sees his access to the opaque, if not entirely hidden, inner chambers of Iran's ruling elite as invaluable. He in turn dances on this fine line, working to serve two masters, an arrangement each of the two parties—the Americans and the supreme leader—perceives, in principle, as being in its interests. Philosophically, Moslehi dreams of the day Iran can reassume the status it enjoyed in the heyday of the shah, when Richard Nixon and Henry Kissinger viewed Iran as the potential hegemon in the Gulf and were building it up to assume the duty of securing the region on behalf of the United States. Today Moslehi is among those Iranian Americans who are working tirelessly to engineer a rapprochement between Iran and the United States, with the hope of ultimately transforming this relationship into a full-fledged alliance. The United States' current alliance with the Gulf Arabs offends him deeply as he believes his beloved Iran, with its large population and old civilization, deserves to be, as the rightful custodian of all Persian Gulf oil, the only appropriate regional counterparty to the United States. When Iran takes over Arabia, he is certain that the US will have little choice but to accept this new reality, and he will be there to ensure that this new alliance is forged to the ultimate benefit of both parties.

Moslehi's normal meeting attire is a tailored suit with a brightly colored necktie. Today, however, he thought it more fitting to forgo the tie, "Iranian Revolution style." While accustomed to being offered a chair when conferring with US officials, his sitting on the floor at the feet of Motahidi does not offend him. Not only does he maintain his affinity for Iranian hierarchy and customs when in Tehran or Qom, but also he appreciates this formal show of respect for and deference to the spiritual and political leader of his mother country. It is in a nation's traditions that its history is best honored, he believes.

"Ayatollah Motahidi," Moslehi begins, respectfully addressing the supreme leader, "here we must realize that while access to Gulf oil is obviously still important to the global economy, it is far less important to the US, and at the same time US public after the Iraq War and Afghanistan has zero appetite for any further military involvement in the region. As a result, the US-Arabian alliance is fundamentally unsound because it is not built on a foundation of American popular support, and this creates opportunities for us that we can eagerly exploit.

"Also, there has been a big change in the American presidential attitude toward the Arab ruling class since the days of the Bush family. They were close to Arab ruling families. 'W,' for example, was a 'prince,' a ruler who was the son of a ruler. He obviously appreciated inherited wealth and power, and because of this he identified with Arab princes. For W, they were all 'Daddy's' personal friends, and he would have reacted very strongly to an Iranian attack on his 'friends.' The Bushes, however, were unique in that regard. Michael Stayer, as president, is a totally different package. A Democrat and a self-made man, he is a product of meritocracy and democracy. He believes in that crap. After all, he is its living embodiment, and hence he has nothing but dislike for Arab autocrats.

The supreme leader from his chair acknowledges this insightful comparison with an appreciative nod of his head.

"Also, let's not forget," Jalili interjects, "that we have today a strong Iranian American community of over two million people. While it is obviously not as potent or influential as the American Jewish community, it is still very active and growing daily in influence. Now, while many Iranian Americans may not support the Islamic Republic, they all support the glory of Iran. Also, and very important to note, they are obsessed with ending Iran's status as a 'demon' in America's eyes since they suffer the embarrassment of that association. In fact, many of them now run around America calling themselves 'Persians' to avoid the correlation." Jalili looks at Moslehi as he makes this derogatory comment, obviously numbering him among that group.

"The job of softening Iran's image, vis-à-vis the American public, is already a key priority for Iranian Americans," Moslehi continues Jalili's line of thought, ignoring his insinuation. "In fact, their efforts have already begun to bear fruit. You will note, for example, the message broadcast over and over in the US media that while the Iranian government is anti-American, 'the Iranian people are the most pro-American people in the Middle East.' Repeat that silly message often enough and it will get into the American subconscious. In fact, a lot of work and effort, including articles, books, lectures, TV programs, and active lobbying, is slowly making an impact, so when Iran attacks the Arabs, the knee-jerk American reaction should not instantaneously be that the Iranians are 'the bad guys attacking our buddies.'

"We are greatly helped here," he continues, glancing around the room at General Rowhani, who is paying only halfhearted attention to him, and at the supreme leader, who is smiling placidly beneath his black turban and behind his white beard, "by the fact that most of the Arab ruling elites still do not fully understand Western democratic politics. They still spend too much time and money focusing on building personal relationships with American leaders rather than on trying to influence American public opinion. They fail to appreciate that for democratic leaders, who obviously need to get reelected, what counts for them is their public's opinion, not any personal connections they may have with these Arabs, however warm those friendships may be. As a result, these elites are constantly disappointed when they are inevitably let down, time and again, by their 'friends' in Washington. This circus has been going on since the 1950s, and many still don't get it. They have no clue as to how tenuous their position actually is with America. It will only hit them when the White House suddenly stops returning their phone calls.

"The Israelis, on the other hand, understand how to influence US public opinion very well. Do you gentlemen realize," Moslehi points out, "that a critical component of shaping American public opinion in favor of Israel in her early days was a novel titled *Exodus*? This book was commissioned by Zionists for the specific purpose of creating a positive American attitude toward Israel. They approached a prominent novelist and worked with him to create a best seller that would present the 'Israeli story' in a manner that would positively appeal to American values and emotions. The project was incredibly successful; it became a blockbuster movie and is now recognized as a case study on how to subtly influence public opinion."

"We, however," Jalili emphasizes, "have studied in great depth how the West operates. Maybe it's easier for us to harbor no illusions since our Islamic Republic never had any friends in the White House anyway!" He snorts. "Now, we obviously recognize that we cannot transform Iran, seen through Western eyes as the 'hostile Islamic Republic' and the 'Iran of the ayatollahs,' into a 'Sweden' in Western perception. That is impossible—and in any event unnecessary. All we need to do is insert into their minds some doubt about us to blunt their instant response to our action as being that of an enemy, thereby causing them to pause and reflect a bit instead of immediately attacking us.

"Here again, we are working very hard with our friends in the Iranian American community to make sure that our story, our point of view, is clearly communicated to the American media, academics, and policy elites so, when the time comes, they will be open to hearing our message. In fact, we are already seeing encouraging results. For example, a book by a former senior CIA official called *The Devil We Know* trashes the Gulf Arabs as weak and unreliable custodians of the world's oil, arguing instead in favor of a US alliance with Iran. Such an extraordinary argument has not been heard in the corridors of Washington since the days of the United States' alliance with the shah."

"This is why," the supreme leader adds, "we decided to drop Qasem Suleimani and reinstate as president Ali Shirazi. Suleimani was stupidly barking at America the whole time, and he unnecessarily soured the Western public's opinion of Iran. He was a loose cannon, one we had to get rid of. Now with Ali Shirazi as president, we are trying to resurrect the illusion of the previous eras, when the West was duped into thinking that a moderate leadership was emerging in Iran. We now keep that old fool busy running around the world, attending interfaith conferences, hugging rabbis, and talking about peace and harmony among civilizations."

"Here," Defense Minister Rowhani adds, "we have also learned the lessons of history from Saddam Hussein and what happened to him when he invaded Kuwait. The Arab sheikhs were very lucky that Saddam was an ignorant thug who had no understanding of global politics. He did not politically prepare the ground before invading. His was a sudden, impetuous decision. For example, in the weeks preceding his attack, he loudly promised to burn Israel, a silly and unnecessary threat that the Israelis used to turn world public opinion against him. He also hanged an English journalist for spying, which obviously caused the world press to revile him. These and other stupid moves later backfired on him, making the job of President George H. W. Bush in generating domestic support and in putting together an international coalition to attack him that much easier. Luckily for the Kuwaitis, Saddam had the political sophistication of a mule. We will not make the same mistake," Rowhani stresses.

"Absolutely," Javad Zarif responds in a firm, self-assured tone of voice, "and here we will also make full use of the Gulf Arab Shia. While most will probably not support us, we have enough of a hard core, particularly among the poorer classes, who will. Not only will these people receive us with open arms as we wreak revenge on their Sunni masters, but also they will provide our invasion with international political cover as we will justify our action as an effort to free them from their oppressors. Our invasion, we will argue, is not an occupation but rather *a liberation of two million Shia*. That is our trump card."

General Zarif is a legendary figure in Iran and throughout the region. As head of the Quds Force, he controls all of Iran's proxies in Lebanon, Iraq, and Afghanistan. Senior Iraqi officials have described him as the most powerful man in Iraq, and even America's generals publicly acknowledge his enormous influence and power. Short and fit with sandy white hair and a lazy right eye, he is a man of few words who is feared and respected within Iran and abroad. His successes in establishing a network in the region and dominating all the complex environments in which he has operated have earned him a special status with the supreme leader, which is evident in his air of self-confidence and barely concealed arrogance. He is to be the driver of this operation, its mastermind and choreographer.

"Here, we will be greatly assisted by our brothers in Iraq who hate the Kuwaitis in particular," Zarif goes on. Jalili and Rowhani exchange a quick glance, overall in agreement with his points but both put off by his overbearing sense of superiority. "The Kuwaitis continue to provoke the Iraqis by insisting they repay their multibillion-dollar Saddam-era debt and make ongoing reparations for the 1990 Iraqi invasion. This while Kuwait is swimming in oil billions! Remember that most Iraqis feel and have always felt that Kuwait belongs to them. And let's not forget, nobody loves a rich cousin, particularly an arrogant one. So we can be sure that the Iraqi public will eagerly support an invasion of Kuwait, particularly if they feel it can succeed.

"In the wider Arab world, we and our ally Hezbollah are continuing to loudly advertise our pro-Palestinian, anti-Zionist posture. Since Palestinians are Sunnis and their cause is still an emotive Sunni cause with the masses, this helps confuse the more gullible Sunnis by blurring our own political agenda in the region."

"We also shall not forget," Jalili adds, "to send a clear message to China, Japan, Korea, and India that their access to Arabian oil will continue under our rule. The supreme leader will confirm this to them, and all efforts will be made to minimize any disruption to the flow of oil. Ultimately it's still the oil that everyone cares about, not the Arabs or the Iranians. Secure their oil, satisfy their needs, and they will happily deal with you."

"Sayed."[8] Khatami enters the discussion, addressing the supreme leader with due respect. "This looks like a very carefully thought-out plan, but it is a plan that nonetheless depends on many assumptions, any facet of which may go wrong. Arab oil has always been a redline for America; what if they go crazy and hit us in Tehran with nuclear weapons? We are taking a gamble that even the Soviet Union in its heyday was unwilling to take. Do we understand the immense risk involved?"

"Your assumption would be correct," Jalili responds out of turn, shocking Khatami, who would never presume to butt in with an answer to a question posed to the supreme leader, "if our invasion is instantly perceived as such a black-and-white issue. In other words, if Iran mounts an overt grab for Arab oil, then, yes, we run that risk. But the whole idea here is to cascade events in a manner that confuses the Americans, which then

---

[8] Many Iranians, while claiming "superiority" over the Arabs, still view the supposed descent from the line of the Prophet Muhammad (an Arab) as the ultimate sign of status and prestige. Such noble descent is designated by the title "Sayed," which Motahidi lays claim to, as do others.

gives us time to establish situations on the ground, in the fog and confusion of war, so that once the Americans wake up to the fact that we have in effect grabbed Arab oil, it will be too late for them to stop us."

Here, Moslehi interjects. "Sir," he politely addresses Khatami, clearing his throat, "a decision to launch nuclear weapons is not one America can make in hours or even days, unless she detects inbound nuclear missiles targeting her homeland or her overseas bases. Introducing nuclear weapons onto a battlefield, for a democracy like America, involves a great deal of debate and consultation, which would require at minimum a few days' time, probably more. After all, such a move would be a huge historic decision resulting in massive civilian casualties. You can be certain that a president would not assume responsibility for such a monumental burden without extensive debate within and substantial consensus among his administration, and also after obtaining strong support from the congressional leadership. It is that time of confusion, indecision, debate, and consensus building that we will use to our advantage. Operation Imam Hussein, its being a joint operation with a US-friendly Iraq, will seriously perplex the Americans. Add to that mix our claim to be moving in to protect the Arab Shia, and we can be assured that this invasion does not hit the US as a black-and-white issue. They will need time to decide, and that is precisely the time we will use to finish our job."

"Fine," Khatami retorts, "that is, in case of a nuclear response. What about a conventional military response? We know the Americans don't have enough troops on the ground and would need months to mobilize in order to strike back against us, but they do have the capacity to mount a serious air and naval attack on Iran by activating the US fleet now stationed in the Gulf."

"Again," Jalili reassures him, "even such an attack would not take place in a knee-jerk fashion. The Americans would need some time to evaluate the situation, and here they will easily conclude that the risk–reward ratio makes no sense for them. They know full well that if they attacked us in a conventional manner, we would unleash a full missile onslaught upon their fleet, on their bases in the Gulf, and also on the oil fields across the region— and we would also mine and close off the Strait of Hormuz. This will shut down the whole Persian Gulf oil industry and bring the global economy to a halt. We will also send hundreds of thousands of troops across the border into Kuwait, Saudi Arabia, and Bahrain. They will have to kill them all, under the ever-watchful gaze of global media. And let's not forget the fact that our men will be mixing in with the local Shia population as well as with Iraqi militias. Will the Americans be ready to massacre all of them? Do they have the stomach for such a war after having pulled out of the region, at least mentally if not physically?

"The Americans would gain little from this and, were they to attack us, would end up provoking global economic chaos that would last months or years. It will make much more sense for them to reach an accommodation with us, which we will eagerly proffer. Would they decide, after careful thought, to fight such a war anyway and create massive chaos just to preserve a few Arab sheikhdoms? Does that add up to you? Why would they choose to pay such a staggering price to defend these rich Arabs if we instead convinced them that the world would receive unfettered access to Arab oil anyway, maybe even at better terms than they have now? All these factors will give them pause. A pause of a few days is all we need, no more."

"But what about their troops in Kuwait," Khatami asks, "and their role as a tripwire?"[9]

---

[9] The "tripwire" is a US concept that had its genesis during the Cold War. It was first applied after the Korean War when the United States placed

Moslehi jumps in to answer this question. "Sir, this is not a concern for us here. First of all, after the removal of Saddam, US forces in Kuwait 'stood down' since their raison d'être as protectors of Kuwait no longer existed. They relocated to camps in remote areas inside the country, away from the border. The role of US military facilities in Kuwait became more of a support area for US troops on their way into and out of the region. A function better described as a supply-chain management and R & R site for any Iraq-based troops or advisors fighting ISIS than as a combat center. We will stay strictly away from their camps. The only circumstance under which we will engage them is if they seek us out, and that will only happen if the political decision is made in Washington that they should do so—and, as previously mentioned, that would take time, enough time for us to meet our objectives. So, all of that said, the tripwire concept here will not apply to the Kuwaiti theater as far as the US is concerned."

"In any event," Rowhani now interjects, "this is a war that once we start, we cannot stop. Our very survival depends on following this military action through to its conclusion. Consequently, our imam has authorized the deployment of hundreds of thousands of potential martyrs to battle." The supreme leader nods in confirmation of the general's statement. "We will force the Americans to face the prospect of killing hundreds of thousands in order to stop us. They will literally have to commit mass

---

troops on the border between South Korea and North Korea to serve the function of a tripwire. The idea here was that if North Korea invaded South Korea, it would have to first go through US forces, engage them, and cause US casualties, which would in turn inflame the US public and generate the necessary public support for the US government to hit back aggressively against the Koreans. The same principle was applied in Berlin during the same period. The concept assumes that it's not the size of the US military troop that counts; rather, it is its simple presence that is important, because attacking *any* US force is enough to provoke a strong US reaction. In Kuwait, the situation is different because US forces are no longer positioned on the border to serve as a tripwire but are instead located in remote areas away from an invader's path.

genocide, and we don't believe that they have the will or the stomach to undertake this type of grand-scale action, which would also be repulsive to many of their allies. They will realize that such a massacre of our men will leave a wound so deep among our people, and among the Shia in general, that it will give birth to a whole new insurgency against them, and believe me, they appreciate our skills in that department.

"Also, such an undertaking in the current world climate of live TV and social media will ignite tremendous debate and dissent among American elites with our friends in America making every effort to create as much noise as possible around this issue. Designed to maximize the projected price America sees that it must pay in order to take us on, it will illuminate the option of reaching an accommodation with us as the most attractive one possible given the circumstances." Rowhani, elbows against his chest, lifts both hands toward Khatami, who is seated directly across from him in the semicircle, in a gesture meant both to persuade and reassure.

After maintaining direct eye contact with the hojatoleslam for an instant, Rowhani resumes speaking, having saved his hardest-hitting rhetoric for last. "Everything we are discussing here boils down to our determination and willingness to pay a high price, if required, to achieve our objectives against a superpower that ultimately will not be defending its land or its own people but rather Arabs, for whom it does not have much affinity anyway. Now, don't misunderstand me, *they certainly will not like the idea of an Iranian empire controlling the world's oil.* They and the British before them have been highly successful in following the divide-and-rule strategy in the Persian Gulf, and with us in control, they will obviously lose that valuable leverage over the world economy. But the question is: *Will it be so unacceptable to them as to force them to pay such a high price to stop us?* That, we believe, is very unlikely.

"For us, the prize is the ultimate supremacy of Iran and Shia Islam, something that has eluded our people since the murder of Imam Hussein. If we succeed, we not only will have saved the Islamic Republic from possible destruction, but we will also make the Iranian empire a world power and ensure the dominance of the Shia faithful over the hated Sunnis. Is that not worth any sacrifice?"

"Hojatoleslam," the supreme leader says, taking up this thread of discussion and adding his own viewpoint to Jalili's, Moslehi's, and Rowhani's in an effort to quell Khatami's very real fears, "any such operation entails some risk, and we all know that the unexpected can always occur. However, our first and foremost point is that *we have little choice*. Should we fail to act, we will all be faced with the likely collapse of our regime. We have no other solution if the Islamic Republic is to survive. I think our people have thought this through very well, and our chances of success are very high. Second, you underestimate divine support. The Almighty will bless us in this noble and holy cause, and God willing, we will be rewarded with success."

At this last comment, Khatami is effectively silenced, making no further argument.

Javad Zarif then concludes the meeting by stating, "What we will need is the right trigger, an outrageous provocation against the Shia that will provide us with the justification for attacking Kuwait. We are covertly preparing that provocation to take place in Kuwait City itself. It is scheduled for the evening of October eleventh, on the holy day of Ashura."

Chapter 2: Israel Cannot Survive

In my opinion, in the next fifteen years we will either see Israel surviving or we will see the end of the Zionist dream. We have fifteen years and no more. We are coming toward the end of the State of Israel.[10]

—Professor Arnon Soffer, chair of geostrategy, University of Haifa

In the year 20XX, "peace" with the Palestinians, the much discussed "two-state solution," is going nowhere despite years of talk, activity, and noise by the participants. The real reason for this stalemate, the proverbial elephant in the room, is one that no Israeli government can, or will, publicly acknowledge: Israel as a *Jewish state* cannot survive unless it ethnically cleanses itself of its minority Palestinian Arab population. The "two-state solution" will not solve this problem for the Israelis since it provides the Arabs with their Palestinian state but leaves Israel with only a temporary Jewish majority, which, in time, will dissolve in a sea of rapidly reproducing Israeli Arab[11] citizens

---

[10] Jonathan Cook, 2001 interview with Arnon Soffer, *Blood and Religion: The Unmasking of the Jewish and Democratic State* (London: Pluto Press, 2006), 135.

[11] Palestinians are Arabs, as are Jordanians and all the inhabitants of the Arabian Peninsula. The Palestinian minority in Israel are also called Israeli

and Palestinians in the surrounding territories. To survive as a *Jewish state*, Israel will need to get rid of its Arabs, but in this politically correct day and age, no state can openly acknowledge that it "doesn't want" a minority, any minority, let alone one that constitutes over 20 percent of its citizenry. That attitude went out of fashion, at least publicly, with the führer and his cohorts. So, Israelis continue to play the slow game of "peace talks," a game they have learned to play very well, as they grapple with how to solve their Arab minority problem.

Caesarea, Israel
6:30 p.m., Tuesday, August 30

It is the end of August as Mordechai Peled, Israel's defense minister, sits on the terrace of Prime Minister Benjamin Leiberman's luxury villa in Caesarea, waiting for the rest of the group to assemble. At the close of an uncharacteristically leisurely day for Peled, he gazes out at the sun setting over the majestic Roman aqueduct that runs down to the Mediterranean Sea in front of him, pondering what he and the others are about to discuss. The prime minister had asked him to drop by his villa to informally review Operation King David, a secret plan to secure the future of the State of Israel, with two other of Leiberman's close advisors. The plan is set to be presented tomorrow to the security cabinet, and Leiberman wants to make sure he has all bases covered before that critical meeting.

Peled, a short, stocky man in his early seventies, nicknamed "the penguin" by friends, is a tough former general known for his phenomenal intellect and just as phenomenal lack of charm. He is a Zionist of the "muscular" persuasion, a fervent believer in the concept of the "new Jew," the strong, powerful, and, if necessary, brutal Jew who can and will fight rather than suffer quietly like the frightened and intimidated caricature of the Jew

---

Arabs, meaning that they are Palestinian Arabs who hold Israeli citizenship.

in European history. He is a cynic, a realist who has no time for idealists who search for the "inner good" in their fellow man. He knows that man, despite having acquired a thin veneer of civility over the course of centuries of progress and prosperity, remains at his core an animal, a savage, with his raw instincts of greed, bigotry, and cruelty still firmly intact. Peled is, after all, a student of history, not the history of textbooks but that of the raw, painful emotions belonging to one who is but a generation beyond the Holocaust.

Born to a Polish woman who escaped Nazi Europe and who had lost her family at Auschwitz, Peled remains outraged that Gentiles still fail to grasp the immense fear and paranoia that Jewish people feel about the world around them. After all, two thousand years of pogroms in Christendom had culminated for Jews in a Holocaust at the epicenter of "enlightened" Western civilization. It had been led by the nation of Goethe, Hegel, and Mendelssohn, where Jews thought they had finally achieved the security of complete assimilation. This was not a pogrom of wild ignorant mobs let loose by events beyond anyone's control. This was genocide carried out in an organized, systematic, industrial manner by their fellow Europeans.

Meanwhile, the Americans, the British, and the rest of the "civilized" world, while making sympathetic noises, did little but close their doors to desperate Jewish emigrants. After the war, it served everybody's purpose, including that of a *politically opportunistic Israel*, to blame everything exclusively on Adolf Hitler and his fellow Nazis. But Zionists like Peled knew better. They knew that the Holocaust succeeded thanks to the acquiescence and even active assistance of vast swaths of the European populace. After the war, when the horror was exposed in all its revolting detail, Europeans reacted by colluding in a mass breakout of collective amnesia and silence. As a result, the Peleds of this world are no longer in a mood to take the goodwill of their fellow humans on faith. This planet they now know is a jungle: the strong survive and the weak don't; it's as brutally simple as that. For Peled, the Zionist has to take Jewish destiny into his own hands, the strong hands of the new Jew: a mighty, militarized, and aggressive Jew, not the meek, pathetic figure that was led quietly to his death in the concentration camps of Europe.

While US neoconservatives continue to espouse militaristic solutions to political problems, the vast majority of Western elites continue to believe that in this post–Cold War era, reasonable solutions to all major political problems can be found. A world of multilateralism, global trade, human rights, and new media is, they are convinced, a world rich in possibilities for the betterment of humankind. There is no political problem, they believe, that can't ultimately be solved in a civilized, mature manner within the overall structure of a modern globalized system of law and order. This naivete, born out of the current unprecedented era of postwar global peace and prosperity, colors their thinking, particularly that of the American centrists and liberal elites, and hence it has to be humored.

The Zionists, while having paid lip service to those comfortable illusions, know otherwise. They are victims and students of humankind's long, painful, and bloody history. They know that the game with the Palestinians *can only be a zero-sum game.* Only one people will ultimately survive in historic Palestine, known to them as Eretz Israel, and Zionists like Peled are here to make damned sure it is the Jews who do the surviving.

Peled arrived early for the meeting at Leiberman's villa, and for the past half hour he has been enjoying the mild late summer weather, gathering his thoughts amid a refreshing salty breeze. He hears the other two men being welcomed inside. The prime minister has invited, in addition to Peled, David

Halevy, Leiberman's unofficial senior advisor and confidant, and Professor Ariel Safran, chairman of the history department at Hebrew University and Israel's paramount expert on Palestinian demographics. Leiberman greets the men in the high-ceilinged foyer as Efraim, the butler, takes their jackets.

Halevy, well into his seventies, is a Zionist of the polished school—urbane, sophisticated, and highly attuned to Western elite opinion. Born to a father who was a don at Cambridge and a mother who hailed from an aristocratic German Jewish banking family, he was educated at Eton and went on to earn a degree in politics, philosophy, and economics at Oxford. Thereafter, bewitched by the dream of Zionism being realized in Palestine, he decided to immigrate to a newly created Israel and join a kibbutz, where he met his wife and settled down. His career had taken him through the ranks of the Mossad, until he became its head of European operations; then he made a jump into politics as a member of the Knesset for the Likud; and he finally capped a brilliant career as Israel's ambassador to the United Nations. Halevy's time in New York had introduced him to the United States' Jewish elite, an experience that forged his strong ties with, and provided him invaluable insight into the views of, Israel's most important Diaspora community. Today, as a wise senior statesman, his ego is well buttressed by his widely recognized status as Leiberman's "consigliere."

Professor Ariel Safran is a giant in two ways: first, within the Israeli academic establishment, where his apocalyptic views on Israel's demographic dilemma were first developed, and second, because he is physically imposing and grossly overweight. A native-born Sabra, he singlehandedly created the field of Israeli demographic studies by spending his career modeling the future trends of Israel's Jewish and Arab populations. He has carefully studied reproduction rates and currents within these different segments of Israel's population, and he continues to game different scenarios in an effort to determine how Israel can retain a Jewish majority and ensure that it ultimately does not become inundated by the sea of Arabs among and around it.

Safran is somewhat frazzled and excuses himself to use the restroom, where he attempts to both gather his composure and smooth the creases in his dark linen shirt. Having traveled to Caesarea from his farm in the Negev, Safran feels dry and dusty, stinking of cigarette smoke.

Leiberman and Halevy wait together in the foyer for Safran's return from the lavatory. David steals a glance at his well-built friend, who still manages, in his sixties, to maintain the physique and arrogant posture of the elite paratrooper he once was. Halevy is, of course, very well acquainted with the background and views of the man standing with him. Leiberman is a Zionist of the Jabotinsky School, which adheres to the "iron wall" ideology of its namesake, who, as early as the 1920s, harbored no illusions that the Arab majority in Palestine would voluntarily accept a Jewish state in their land. For Jabotinsky, a Jewish state in Palestine could only be established by brute force, and it would only survive and be able to prosper behind an iron wall of military strength that Arabs could never pierce. He had no illusions that a consensual arrangement could ever be reached with an indigenous population to give up its country to foreign colonizers. And indeed, this outlook had permeated Leiberman's mission in life. His late father had after all been a Jabotinsky disciple. And Leiberman himself is now determined to finally put in place that very iron wall his idol had insisted on, to ensure the future of his people as uncontested owners of their "ancestral land."

Upon Safran's reemergence, Leiberman walks both men to the terrace, and the three take their seats near Peled. These members of Israel's ruling class, its self-confident elite, are now here to discuss their country's survival, which they recognize is seriously in doubt. The swagger—arrogance, even—that they often project onto the world stage hides a deep, nagging unease that, every so often, makes them break out in a cold sweat of fear. Israel, they all continue to worry, will not be able to survive as a Jewish state.

Efraim takes their orders and, after a brief delay inside, reenters the terrace with a tray of fruit and drinks. Halevy admires the view and good-naturedly teases Leiberman about living in Israel's most exclusive residential community. "Ben-Gurion must be rolling over in his grave," he jokes. "Here you are the leader of a country created by socialists, yet you get away with living in exclusive luxury, neighbor to a Russian billionaire and the Baron de Rothschild. Zionists invented the kibbutz, but you patronize a California-style gated community of millionaires."

Leiberman takes a sip of his beer and responds to Halevy's jibe. "Well, we have all come a long way." He smiles awkwardly. "After all, Israel has certainly come a long way!" The men then marvel at Israel's great progress since the dream of a Jewish state was born in 1897 at the First Zionist Congress in Basel. It was to become a reality in Palestine only fifty years later, and now Israel has made itself into a military, economic, and technological power with vast global influence. This achievement is nothing short of miraculous—so miraculous, they muse, chuckling, that even to some secular Zionists it has become an article of faith that Zionism is in the miracle business. For the men assembled, however, faith in miracles is a luxury they are not willing to bet on.

Their nightmare is Palestinian population growth, that "cancer" rapidly spreading among them, which Professor Safran has publicly argued will have to be expunged if their young state is ever to have a chance at survival. "Let me lay out the parameters of the demographic disaster that awaits us," Safran begins, once setting down his coffee and lighting a cigarette. "Today, over 20 percent of Israel's seven million citizens are the descendants of the Palestinian Arabs who managed to avoid being expelled in the 1948 war.[12] They were able to do this on account of a major strategic mistake that Ben-Gurion made when he prematurely stopped the 1948 War of Independence and thus failed to finish the job of ejecting all the indigenous Arabs from Eretz Israel. He got cold feet and did not want to upset the Great Powers at that time. We have been paying the price for that huge mistake ever since. In fact, not only have those Arabs remained in Israel, but also we have had to give them Israeli citizenship and hence 'the vote.' These 'Israeli Arabs' are now reproducing at a higher rate than the Israeli Jews, and they are consequently projected to exceed a third of our population in coming years."

Now, within his comfort zone of theory, statistics, and analysis, Safran's previous edginess is gone. He continues, "Remember that we insist on defining Israel as the 'Jewish state.' By that definition, then, the Arabs among us are obviously disenfranchised. After all, our national anthem mentions only Jews, the law of return applies only to Jews, and even our Independence Day celebrates our victory over the Arabs." The three other men nod in recognition. "All our important leaders are Jewish, every single president, prime minister"—he cocks his head at Leiberman—"key cabinet minister, and general," he says, gesturing with his cigarette in Peled's direction, "is and has always been a Jew. We have never even bothered to elect or appoint a token Arab to any of these key positions. This in a democracy that is supposed to guarantee all its citizens equal

---

[12] Called by Israelis the War of Independence and by Palestinians the Nakba (Disaster), it is the war in which Jewish immigrants took control of most of the land of Palestine and established a Jewish state. This war led to the expulsion of a majority of Palestinians. Those who were able to remain, in the new State of Israel, are today called "Israeli Arabs" and constitute 20 percent of the Israeli population.

rights. This harsh reality reinforces the Israeli Arab's deep sense of bitterness and anger at being treated as an alien in his land. Now history teaches us that such feelings are inevitable with a defeated people. We must realize that *unless such people are uprooted or annihilated, they never forget.* In their closed ethnic communities, they preserve and reinforce this sense of anger and humiliation—and they nurture their fury until it explodes. Such minorities can and do cause state breakdowns. It is only a matter of time. We can't ignore this time bomb within us.[13]

"Even today," Safran goes on, "Arabs constitute over 30 percent of the zero-to-nine-year age group in this country. That is the immediate future staring us in the face. Let me also remind you gentlemen that these figures are actually worse than they seem since they conceal a painful fact, namely that close to a million Israelis now live abroad, mainly in the US and Europe. We have thirty thousand Israelis living in Berlin. For God's sake, Berlin! Don't our people have any shame? What's more, the trend is growing as many European governments, presumably to assuage their guilt about their role in history, are now presenting Israelis with residence and citizenship on a silver platter. To make matters worse, those who emigrate are inevitably the best educated and most ambitious since such people are by nature the most mobile and can most easily find jobs and resettle abroad. Finally, we can hardly rely on fresh Jewish immigration into Israel, because Jews in recent decades have overwhelmingly voted with their feet and gone to America or Europe instead of Israel when given a choice.

"Now, when they reach 30 percent of our population, Arabs will no longer be a minority in the conventional sense of the term. Given our fractured society, they can, in fact, become the largest political bloc in this country. Israelis are already divided along

---

[13] An example of such thinking can be seen in a blog, by an anonymous Israeli political figure, found at www.samsonblinded.org.

community lines—Ashkenazi, Sephardic/Mizrahi, Russian, Orthodox, liberal, et cetera—in addition to the lines between all our political parties. If these Arabs get organized, or rather *when* they get organized, they will be by far the largest, most cohesive bloc in the country and as such could very well come to control our political system. If Israel is to retain her democratic system of government—that is, if we continue to give these people the vote, *which is obviously essential to preserving our 'democratic' image in the West*—these Arabs will gradually be able to work through the system and destroy Zionism. They will become capable of dismantling the Jewish state silently, from within, using the respectable and totally legitimate tools of democracy. All they will need to do, for example, is overturn the 'law of return.'" This law today allows a Jew who never lived in Israel, theoretically a descendant of a Jew who left Palestine two thousand years ago, to "return," but it refuses to readmit an Arab who was born here decades ago—or to admit his children. "If this law alone is amended to give equal rights to the Arabs, then millions of them will come in, and we will be finished. In fact, Arabs and Israeli leftists are already petitioning the Israeli Supreme Court for this very thing. Today we ignore them, but for how long can we continue getting away with this?"

While Safran has been speaking, Peled has been observing Leiberman. More than four decades have passed since Peled was Leiberman's commanding officer in the Sayeret Matkal, an elite special forces unit of the Israel Defense Forces, yet Peled sometimes still struggles to fully accept that his former subordinate is now his superior.

Safran takes a moment to sip his coffee, spilling a few drops onto his shirt. He then goes on: "Ultimately, if we become a minority ourselves, we will end up in a new Jewish ghetto among the Arabs. That will be the end of Zionism and eventually even of the Jews in their ancestral land. It's that simple! And let's not forget that we have considered all the tricks of the trade to try to control this problem. We have offered Jews all sorts of incentives to procreate and have looked at many ideas to push the Arabs to emigrate or reduce their birth rate. Nothing has worked, so the bottom line is that we simply cannot afford to keep these Arabs among us, living and breeding like rabbits, until they destroy us.

"Now, if that problem in and of itself were not enough," Safran continues, having stubbed out his first and lit a second cigarette, an aura of smoke around his head, "it gets worse when you factor in the impact of the 1967 war and our occupation of the West Bank and Gaza. That occupation has saddled us with another four million Arabs. When you add them into the pot of our one and a half million Arab citizens, you see that Arabs immediately become half the population in Eretz Israel. So whether we withdraw from the occupied territories or not, we will lose our Jewish majority anyway. It's just a question of time. Either way, we lose."

"Even then," Peled jumps in, "the problem is not completely solved, since we still have to deal with the 'right of return' of the five million Palestinian refugees living outside Israel and in the occupied territories. Any new Palestinian state in these territories will continue to insist on the right of return of these refugees to their homes, most of which are in Israel. Even in the unlikely event that the Palestinians give up this right and the new Palestinian state absorbs them instead, it could conceivably end up squeezing another five million Arabs into that small strip of land between the Jordan River and the sea that we share with all of them. Eventually the Arabs in the Palestinian state and in Israel will overwhelm us by sheer demographic pressure. This will lead to civil disobedience, more intifadas, and ultimately armed insurrection. Any way you look at this issue, we are cooked. *There is no peaceful solution to sharing this land with the Arabs. It's either them or us.*"

"We are all familiar," Leiberman comments, "with these arguments and have been discussing and debating them for years—decades, even. Now we are running out of time. We need to take action. We have international pressure piling up on us to solve the 'Palestinian problem.' Populism is reemerging in the Arab world, which is inevitably hostile to Israel, so the cozy days of cutting deals with Arab dictators are over. The Palestinians have seen the power of nonviolent protest at work in the Arab revolutions; they are learning that lesson and are now applying that strategy against us. Look at the emerging power and success of the BDS movement despite all we have done to try to stop it. The regional and global environment is becoming more hostile toward us. We can no longer claim to be the only democracy in the Middle East given the emergence of these new Arab democracies. We also can no longer camouflage our subjugation of the Palestinians; in fact, people are increasingly describing Israeli policies as apartheid."

Leiberman continues, "At the same time, we have to realize that we cannot continue spending such a huge percentage of our GNP on the military forever. That policy eventually destroyed even the Soviet Union. Let's also not forget that we now survive with the help of massive American aid. That will not last forever either. America can hardly pay its own debt, and it's only a matter of time before the US public begins to question the financial and military aid that we depend on. All this means that our military strength, which is massive, as we are probably the third or fourth most powerful military in the world, needs to be used now, while we still have that advantage. In the future, we may not be able to afford to maintain this level of strength. Israel is slowly and surely being strangled at all levels. Time is working against us, and the longer we delay taking action, the lower our chance of success will ultimately be. We have to make our move now."

Halevy weighs this last comment while slightly adjusting the tie expertly knotted at his throat. *How on earth,* he ponders, *will we ever get rid of this miserable Palestinian problem?*

"This is why," Safran urges, pounding his index finger on the tabletop, "the only realistic final solution to retaining a Jewish-majority state in perpetuity is to kick out the Arabs, *all* the Arabs, from Eretz Israel—and do it now." He locks eyes with each of the others, pausing a moment to let the force of his statement sink in. Then he concedes, "This is not pretty, let's not kid ourselves; it is ugly, very ugly, but we have no choice. Fifty years from now, only one people will be left here: either the Arabs or us.[14] Let's have no illusions about that."

"Now, gentlemen," Peled interjects, "we all know that Israel has one supreme military advantage, and that is our regionally exclusive nuclear arsenal. It has given us some comfort and created an illusion of invincibility among our people, and it affords us the power to impose a final military solution on the region. However, the minute we lose that monopoly, we are finished since we can never survive a nuclear attack. We are a 'one bomb' state today. We cannot play the game of 'mutually assured destruction' that the USA and the Soviets played for fifty years. Israel has no territorial or human strategic depth like the superpowers do, each with a large continent and hundreds of millions of people to survive a first strike. For Israel, all it takes is one bomb dropped on Tel Aviv, and the game is over for Zionism. For the Arabs or Iranians, this is a game they can afford to play given the vast territories and millions of people at their disposal. Also, if you factor in the Islamist element,

---

[14] An example of this thinking is evident in a comment by Professor Benny Morris of Ben-Gurion University who is a prominent member of what are called the "new historians" in Israel: "In fifty or a hundred years there will only be one state between the sea and the Jordan. That state must be Israel." Quoted by Norman G. Finkelstein in *Image and Reality of the Israel-Palestine Conflict,* 2nd ed. (London: Verso, 2003), xxix.

and the possibility that one of these countries may eventually come under the rule of an Islamic leadership that will operate as an existential gambler willing to lose millions of its people to destroy us—an 'Islamist Stalin,' for example—then the risk becomes even more deadly. Consequently, the day that any of these states goes nuclear is the day the countdown to Israel's demise begins. Once we lose the nuclear monopoly," he stresses, "we are finished."

Peled has been carefully dividing an orange into sections while speaking. After popping a couple of pieces into his mouth and swallowing quickly, he resumes. "Today, gentlemen, Iran is about to achieve this nuclear parity. Our analysts are unsure as to the exact stage of development of their program, but they all agree that it's very advanced, and Iran's achieving the capacity to build a nuclear weapon is a matter of time, a few years at most. We have to deal with this issue. The UN continues to play cat and mouse with the Iranians, a game the Iranians have mastered, and the Americans just don't have the stomach for another Middle Eastern war. It's as simple as that. They are not going to come in and solve this problem for us. We have to do it ourselves."

Leiberman finishes his beer and motions to Efraim, just inside, to bring another tray of refreshments. *It's going to be a longer night than I thought,* he acknowledges to himself.

"Without the Americans, the only way we can effectively succeed is by using our nuclear weapons," Peled says, wiping a corner of his mouth with a napkin then cleaning juice from his fingers. "Conventional attacks by our air force cannot do it. We don't have the reach or the firepower to deliver such a sustained conventional attack against Iran's facilities. Only the Americans with their airpower in the Gulf can do that. At best, our attacks would be pinpricks that would gain us nothing but would cost us a high price, diplomatically speaking. So we have to do the job with nuclear weapons, specifically our submarine-launched missiles. These will vaporize the main Iranian nuclear sites, the underground facilities, and also the related personnel on-site, potentially their most valuable resource, since rebuilding facilities takes far less time than recreating a highly capable brain trust of scientists and engineers. The time is now," Peled emphasizes, "*to come out of the closet* and use our nuclear weapons. This will also send a clear message to the Iranians and the Arabs that Israel will destroy them before any one of them is *ever* allowed to go nuclear.

"And this attack will serve two other very important purposes. It will provoke Iran and Hezbollah to retaliate and will cause global financial markets to panic as oil prices go through the roof. This will provide us with the cover of regional and global chaos we need to start our war, and by distracting the world's attention, it will give us the time we require to achieve our objectives before the Americans jump on us to stop fighting.

"So, in this fog and confusion of regional war, Israel will explode out of her shackles and solve her Palestinian demographic problem once and for all by forcibly expelling all her Arabs into Jordan. Now is the time," he stresses, "for Israel to gamble everything in her quest to ensure survival. This window will close forever the minute Iran goes nuclear."

"A theoretically compelling argument," Halevy responds, moving aside as Efraim clears his empty glass and sets a fresh one in front of him, "but this is the twenty-first century. Do we have to take such a dangerous gamble and put everything we have created here at risk? Do you gentlemen understand the enormity of this undertaking? The world will be outraged and the Jewish Diaspora deeply embarrassed—and we could become a pariah state, an outlaw state, like North Korea! Are we prepared for that; is that what we want? We have spent decades carefully building up our stature and ties to the international community. We have argued our case very effectively. Even those who oppose us in the West still accept our 'right to exist' as a Jewish state in our ancestral land. Why risk it all?"

"You say this, David," Leiberman answers him, "assuming that time is on our side, but it is not. Demographics and regional political developments are working against us, global political trends are moving against us, and even America's unconditional support for Israel cannot be relied on indefinitely. Let us not become like the frog slowly coming to a boil in a pan that only realizes it is being cooked when it's too late for it to jump out. Failure to act is our biggest risk; in fact, it is not so much a risk as a certainty that such a failure will be akin to signing the death warrant of the Jewish state."

"I don't know," Halevy continues, concern clouding his face. "We operate in a world where such action will never be supported by our allies, the Americans and Europeans. Also, it is certainly not in their best interests for us to set the region aflame, pushing up the price of oil and damaging their economies. After all, the US is a status quo power; they don't want us to drive a bulldozer of destruction through the Middle East."

"But that is the point," Safran barks back. "We cannot be bound by these constraints any longer! Israel cannot be a status quo power. We need to provoke regional and even global chaos to distract the world if we are to succeed in expelling the Palestinians." Blood rushes to Safran's face, sweat droplets forming on his brow. "The status quo is slowly killing us. The Arabs will soon overwhelm us in number, and then our state will be destroyed. *We have no choice.* We need to become, in the words of Moshe Dayan, 'the mad dog' of the region, lashing out wildly at our enemies, destroying them once and for all. Let's stop worrying about our 'image,' and let us please stop listening to the Jewish Diaspora and their liberal friends. There is no elegant solution to our predicament, which is nothing short of the survival of a Jewish state in Palestine. We are on our own. The Jew has always been alone, and we have to act accordingly. Nobody will protect us from destruction, not the Americans and certainly not the Europeans. We cannot afford the pretense of belonging to the club of 'civilized' Western nations, upholding lofty values of human rights and democracy. *That crap you can only afford to practice as a state once you have eliminated the existential threats to your survival, but not before that time.* No people or country fighting for its survival throughout history has given a shit about the welfare or rights of its enemies. They only start to parrot this stuff once they are safe, secure, and in control.

"Look at the sanctimonious Americans lecturing us on Palestinian rights. They who built their country on the bones of the American Indian. Do you gentlemen know," Safran continues, wishing he had asked Efraim to bring him an iced tea now that he has worked up a thirst, "that 95 percent of the indigenous population of the 'New World' was wiped out by the white man? They say it was mostly due to disease, but that's bullshit. As recently as Teddy Roosevelt's time, the ideology of the ruling class in America was built on the concept of 'manifest destiny,' which argued that as 'Teutons'—that is, Aryans—and as the stronger race, they had a duty to exterminate the American Indian and take his land. You can then add to that their shameful track record of slavery and crimes against the American Negro. Who the hell are they to lecture us! These theories of racial superiority were adopted by the whole European race until Hitler and the Holocaust embarrassed and exposed them all. By then, anyway, they had all finished their own ethnic cleansings, including emptying Europe of its Jews, and could afford to take the high ground and wag a finger of disapproval at us as we struggled to survive here in our ancestral homeland. We, at least, have two thousand years of pogroms and the Holocaust driving us in this direction, while their aims were purely greed and glory."

At this point, the prime minister lays his palms flat on the table, looks at each man in turn, and says, "Fine, gentlemen, but the devil is in the details. Let's review our plan."

Chapter 3: Operation King David

With each passing day, the expulsion of the Palestinians grows more probable. The alternative would be total annihilation and disintegration of Israel. What do you expect from us? [15]

—Martin van Creveld, professor of military history, Hebrew University

Caesarea, Israel
8 p.m., Tuesday, August 30

"Operation King David," Defense Minister Peled begins, "is a plan to provoke a regional cataclysmic war [16] and use this war to expel

---

[15] Martin van Creveld, "We Are Destroying Ourselves," interview with Ferry Biedermann, *Elsevier,* April 27, 2002, 52–53.

[16] Here also, the concept of looking at a potential cataclysmic war as an opportunity to effect change on the ground in Israel's favor is touched upon by Professor Benny Morris: "If you are asking me whether I support the transfer and expulsion of the Arabs from the West Bank, Gaza and perhaps even from Galilee and the Triangle [Israel], I say not at this moment. I am not willing to be a partner to that act. In the present circumstances, it is neither moral nor realistic. The world would not allow it, the Arab world would not allow it, it would destroy the Jewish society from within. But I am ready to tell you that *under other circumstances,* apocalyptic *ones, which are liable to be realized in five or ten years, I can see expulsions.* If we find ourselves with

45

the Arabs from all the lands we ultimately want for the State of Israel. We start by attacking Iran's nuclear facilities. When she reacts and her proxies Hezbollah and Hamas retaliate against us, we will have the excuse we need to launch a fierce attack on three fronts: Lebanon, the West Bank–Jordan, and Gaza–Sinai.

"We will hit the Iranians with nuclear missiles." Peled pounds his fist into his hand, pausing for effect, so the others have a moment to absorb this important point. "We focus only on their nuclear facilities, not on their ground troops or navy. Our objective is to cripple their nuclear program, nothing more. Once the Iranians are attacked, they will lash out at the Americans and Gulf Arabs, assuming their complicity with Israel. Iran will transform the Gulf into a blazing inferno. In turn, her clients Hezbollah and Hamas will retaliate by firing their missiles at us. This will provide us with sufficient justification for starting our war.

"We learned in the 2006 war with Hezbollah in Lebanon how easy it is to make civilians flee in conditions of combat. At that time, we successfully pushed half a million Lebanese out of south Lebanon in a matter of days. We are confident that we can duplicate this effect now in the West Bank, Gaza, and south Lebanon, particularly given that this time our hands will not be tied by our usual obsession with world opinion.

"We will also, let us be clear, take action inside the borders of the State of Israel to terrorize all our Arab citizens into fleeing. Fighting inside Israel will be the most delicate part of the operation, so we will need to employ special measures to

---

atomic weapons around us, or if there is a general Arab attack on us and a situation of warfare on the front with Arabs in the rear shooting at convoys on their way to the front, acts of expulsion will be entirely reasonable. They may even be essential" (emphasis mine). Ari Shavit, interview with Benny Morris, "Survival of the Fittest," Haaretz.com, January 9, 2004, http://www. haaretz.com/hasen/spages/380986.html.

camouflage the role of the state. *We have, in fact, gamed and trained for just such a scenario. This exercise took place in October of 2010.*[17] In a five-day drill code-named Warp and Weft, we envisaged large-scale disturbances by Israeli Arabs in reaction to a move by the government to expel them to a new Palestinian state. Among the eventualities the security services trained for was the establishment of a large detention center in the Galilee region between Nazareth and Tiberias to cope with the projected arrest of large numbers of these Arabs. This exercise tested the readiness of civil defense units, police, army, and prison services to deal with such a scenario, and I am pleased to confirm to you that it all went exactly to plan. The Israeli media, with the exception of that troublesome Carmela Menashe of Israeli Radio, hardly mentioned this exercise, and the only commentary on the topic in the Knesset was a typical criticism raised by Dov Chenin of the Communist Party. Even the US media completely ignored it.

---

[17] "Israel secretly staged a training exercise [in October 2010] to test its ability to quell any civil unrest that might result from a peace deal that calls for the forcible transfer of many Arab citizens, the Israeli media has reported. The drill was intended to test the readiness of the civil defence units, police, army and prison services to contain large-scale riots by Israel's Arab minority in response to such a deal. Details of the five-day drill were reported ... on the Voice of Israel radio station by Carmela Menashe, one of Israel's most respected military correspondents.

"The exercise envisioned extensive disturbances by Israel's Arab citizens, one-fifth of the population, as security forces prepared to enforce border changes that would forcibly relocate many to a new Palestinian state, according to her report.

"In the operation, code-named Warp and Weft, the security services established a large detention centre in the Galilee region between Nazareth and Tiberias to cope with an 'unprecedented' number of arrests of Arab citizens." Jonathan Cook, "Israeli Forces Train for Arab Transfer Riots," *The National,* October 14, 2010, accessed December 20, 2011, http://www.thenational.ae/news/worldwide/middle-east/israeli-forces-train-for-arab-transfer-riots.

"Now, while we have to be careful within our borders, outside the official borders of the State of Israel, in Hezbollah's south Lebanon and in the West Bank and Gaza, we can and will attack the Arabs mercilessly.

"The fundamental point here, gentlemen, is that we will no longer occupy land and allow indigenous peoples to remain on it. Israel has learned her lesson from history the hard way. Now we take land *after* we empty it of its people.

"First we explode into Lebanon and rid Southern Lebanon of Hezbollah and its Shia community. Then we attack and expel all the Arabs living in Israel and the occupied West Bank and Gaza, and we also reoccupy the Sinai Peninsula. We do this quickly, without constraints. Frankly, freed from our previous concerns about civilian casualties and our 'image' in the world, we can accomplish this in a matter of days. The Arabs won't know what hit them. The West and China will be so overwhelmed by the collapse of global financial markets that they will be too distracted to even try to stop us. As for the Russians, well, they will be laughing all the way to the bank as their oil revenues shoot up.

"In south Lebanon," Peled explains, "it is vital that we finish off Hezbollah permanently. They are an organization that feeds on war; in fact, they can only survive with continuous war. We will never have peace as long as they're around, since they will keep stirring the pot against us for as long as they can. To destroy them, we need to first understand that they have turned their Shia cadres into the 'Prussians' of the Arab world. This is the most disciplined and most ideologically committed Arab military we now face or have ever faced, for that matter. We cannot beat Hezbollah by destroying a few of their missiles and killing a few of their soldiers every few years. We need to drain the swamp that breeds them, and that is the Shia population of south Lebanon. We have to wipe that community completely out of south Lebanon and force their dispersal into hostile territory, namely, the Sunni, Christian, and Druze regions of Lebanon. Only then will Hezbollah be effectively finished. If any remnants of it survive this attack, we can then be sure that the other sects of Lebanon, who all detest Hezbollah, will eventually finish them off." Peled squeezes an apricot between his thumb and forefinger, its tender flesh rupturing through its skin, to punctuate his statement.

"We then take advantage of this opportunity to annex south Lebanon up to the Litani River." Peled uses his four fingers to draw a line in the air, indicating the expanse across Lebanon to the Mediterranean Sea. "This will give us possession of the waters of the Litani, which we have always wanted as our ultimate northern border. In fact, Chaim Weizmann tried as far back as 1930 to convince the British and the French to accept this river as our border, arguing, maybe with some humor, that 'Lebanon was already well watered.' In any event, our water requirements are now much more acute than they were projected to be back then. And by annexing south Lebanon, we get the added bonus of capturing her newly discovered offshore gas reserves.

"In pushing the Palestinians into Jordan, we will have to destroy Jordan's military and security backbone. This will serve the dual purpose of preventing the Jordanians from obstructing the exodus of Palestinians into Jordan while also terminally weakening the 'East Bank' Jordanian elite, for whom the armed forces constitute the foundation of power. This will then allow the numerically emboldened Palestinians to take over Jordan, with our support and encouragement, and create their 'Palestinian state.' We made a huge mistake in the 1969 Jordanian civil war when we failed to support Arafat and the PLO in their attempt to take over Jordan. Golda Meir should have listened to Ariel

Sharon and dumped the Hashemite monarchy, but instead she stupidly protected King Hussein because he was a 'nice guy' and had always cooperated with us."

"Here, Golda missed the fundamental point," Safran points out excitedly, invigorated by Peled's incisive outline of the operation, "which is that Jordan is the only viable and natural 'home' for all the Palestinians. Our Zionist forefathers recognized that early on, and in fact Weizmann proposed that exact idea to the British. Allowing Jordan, as it is configured today, to continue to exist serves no Israeli purpose inasmuch as it keeps the Palestinians bottled up in Israel, Gaza, and the West Bank. Jordanian East Bank elites have bullied the Hashemites into creating a state wherein a few East Bank families have become the privileged class with exclusive access to state patronage, funded by the Palestinian majority with their taxes and remittances sent home from working in the Gulf. The Jordanians even use a color-coded system to designate a Palestinian's 'class' of citizenship, as in green, yellow, pink, which assigns each class different residency, labor, and property ownership rights. Also, Jordan's rulers now not only are refusing to allow any more Palestinians to settle in Jordan, but also are even trying to push some out, all in fear of this Palestinian demographic threat. Why should we care about this privileged minority? If Arafat had taken over Jordan, the Palestinians would have then had a country. This would have completely eliminated the pressure placed on us to create a Palestinian state in our land. Our job now is to finally correct that historical mistake," Safran exclaims.

"Do away with a regime that has been our only real Arab ally from as far back as the 1920s," Halevy interrupts, "a regime that cooperated with us in establishing our state in the 1948 war and has worked diligently since that time to preserve security along the border we share with them? What message are we sending to potential Arab allies if we flush the Hashemites and their allies down the toilet so easily?"

"Well," Peled retorts, "we all know that there are no permanent friends in politics, only interests. The Jordanians may have served a purpose in the past, but their strategic usefulness to us ended years ago. Today the Jordanian state stands in the way of the only viable permanent solution to the Palestinian problem and hence to Israel's secure future. We cannot put the future of our people at risk because we owe 'loyalty' to a regime that cooperated with us in the past. They did so, after all, with their own selfish interests in mind, not because of our blue eyes. Let's not forget that our support has been a critical factor in their survival for over sixty years, so they were very well rewarded for their services."

"I agree with Mordechai," Safran adds, addressing Halevy. "The reason the Palestine issue has been festering for all these decades is that the Palestinians were never fully integrated and assimilated into any Arab country. What has kept this miserable issue alive are the millions of refugees rotting in camps all over the region, eliciting world sympathy and breeding extremism. This did not have to happen. Look at the example of successful population transfers after World War One between Greece and Turkey and of those between Pakistan and India after partition. And don't forget what happened to ethnic Germans after the war. Thirty million were uprooted from their homes in Central Europe and sent to Germany in the largest, most brutal mass expulsion in history. All these 'transfer' programs ultimately succeeded because those refugees were fully assimilated into their adopted countries. After all, we assimilated the whole wash of Arab Jews who came here from Iraq, Yemen, and Morocco. The Arabs, however, kept and still keep millions of Palestinians stuck in miserable camps and afford them only refugee status. We have to realize by now that we cannot successfully kill this issue unless we force Palestinian assimilation down the Arabs' throats, and that is possible only in Jordan because they are already the majority there. We will give Palestinians control of Jordan and make sure they rule it. They will then absorb *all* Palestinians, not only ours but also those coming to them from Lebanon, Syria, Egypt, and elsewhere. Believe me, we will be solving a huge problem for the whole region, not just for ourselves. This problem has been festering for so long, like a perpetual sore, that even the Arabs want to see closure on it. The world community, after some initial grumbling, will recognize our actions as the perfect solution to this otherwise never-ending issue and ultimately come to accept it."

"We will also reoccupy Sinai," Peled elaborates. "Today our peace treaty with Egypt is not worth the paper it's written on. Egyptian public opinion is anti-Israeli, and the democratically elected government is again dominated by the Muslim Brotherhood and is reneging on key terms of this treaty. They strongly support Hamas in Gaza, refuse to sell us the gas they promised, and barely deal with us diplomatically. Since our decision to return Sinai to the Egyptians was predicated on Egypt's continuing cooperation, why should we stick to our side of the deal now that they've backtracked? In fact, what's happened in Egypt exposes the bankruptcy of our previous strategy of cutting deals with Arab elites who have no popular legitimacy. Populism is flowing across the region, and Arab populism is by definition anti-Israeli. Since current ruling elites are vulnerable and Arab democracies will not accept us, trying to work with the Arabs now is useless. So let's do what we have to do, once and for all. Peace with Egypt has become an expensive joke for us."

"Well, not entirely a joke, my friends," Halevy reminds the men. "It eliminated Egypt as a military threat, and it also secured Egypt's de facto consent to our continued occupation of the West Bank. This allowed us to attack Lebanon and oust the PLO in 1982—and also to squeeze Hamas in Gaza for decades. Now, although it is a given that the government that recently replaced the military dictatorship is less cooperative, it *is* democratically elected, so any deal we cut with them will be much more stable than one we cut with a dictator. Also, a Muslim Brotherhood in power is different from one in opposition. This time around they have to rule Egypt and satisfy their voters, instead of screwing up like they did last time, something they paid a very heavy price for. They have to deliver prosperity to their people, and to do that they will need peace, just like Sadat, Mubarak, and Sisi did. Let's wait and see; maybe we can reach an accommodation with them. Egypt is a land of more than a hundred million people, the most important Arab country; you cannot disregard its importance like that. You will be kicking a hornet's nest by attacking them, and you will cause eternal conflict if you grab their land as well."

"Look, David," Peled responds impatiently, "we have to approach Israel's future security in a radically different manner. *We need to engineer a paradigm shift in the way the Arabs perceive us.* Whatever concessions we make will never satisfy them all. They will continue to be pissed off about something. If it's not the West Bank, it's Gaza. If not Gaza, it's some border village in Lebanon. If not Lebanon, it's Jerusalem. If not all that, it's our Israeli Arabs." He leans forward in Halevy's direction, raising his eyebrows for emphasis. "We will never be able to solve all the problems we have with them, *never get them to forgive, forget, and accept us* as a happy member of the regional family. We may reach an agreement with an Arab government, but then a new demagogue can pop out somewhere else and use us as the perfect scapegoat with which to inflame Arab masses all over again, and then we are back to square one. Just like we are with Egypt now. What we need to do instead is fundamentally change the way the Arabs come to terms with our presence among them. *Peace with Israel has to be seen as the price the Arabs have to pay for survival, as a people and as nations.* Peace cannot be the 'gift' they graciously extend to us if only we agree to every single one of their demands. Instead, *they have to stare nuclear holocaust in the face* and realize that either they capitulate and accept us unconditionally as a Jewish state and recognize our newly expanded borders, or else we will incinerate them. That has to be their risk–reward calculation, and the Arab masses need to clearly understand this."

Even while disturbed by the discomforting details of Operation King David, Halevy notes that when worked up, Peled does indeed resemble a penguin.

"Why should we accept anything less?" Peled demands. "Today we have awesome power. Not only is our military among the top four in the world, but also we lay claim to one of the most sophisticated nuclear weapons capabilities on earth plus the sixth-largest arsenal of nuclear weapons on the globe. We have spent over fifty years and billions of dollars developing this capability, building the most advanced delivery systems and warheads, including low-yield tactical nukes. We are also, gentlemen, probably the number one cyberpower in the world[18]— number one! That is something very few people realize. We command all this power and retain tremendous global political influence, and yet we allow ourselves to be slowly bled to death by the Arabs? Let us use this power, let the Arabs and the rest of the world realize that we can and will use our power, all of it, and let them have no other choice but to reconcile themselves to the outcome." Peled sits back in his chair, feeling less indignant now that he has affirmed his analyses. "We are not going to allow ourselves to be squeezed into a tiny sliver of a state surrounded by hostile Arabs and watch Arab demographics slowly eat us from within while hostile nuclear powers emerge to threaten us

---

[18] "Address by PM Netanyahu at the Graduation Ceremony of Course 38 of the National Security College," [Israeli] Prime Minister's Office, July 25, 2011, accessed November 25, 2011, http://www.pmo.gov.il/PMOEng/Communication/PMSpeaks/speechmbl250711.htm.

and we but meekly await our inevitable demise. This is the first chance in two thousand years for Jews to have a state to protect them, and we blow that chance?" He dismissively shakes his head. "Frankly, gentlemen, if we fail to act today as the leaders of Israel, we deserve damnation until the end of time."

Halevy rubs the stem of his wineglass, uncomfortable with the force of Peled's convictions, which to him smack of hubris.

Peled elaborates, "In fact, if we fail to take action soon, the end of Israel may come much more quickly than many think. Our people already sense our vulnerability and have started voting with their feet. Why do you think Jewish immigration to Israel has virtually stopped and many of our dynamic youth are leaving Israel to settle abroad? They already sense impending doom. We have to arrest the feeling that is spreading among them, and among the Diaspora, before it's too late. A Jewish superpower, omnipotent, strong, and vibrant, will attract Jews to come and settle. We want to re-create the excitement and pride that brought Jews to Israel in the early days and that so energized immigration after the 1967 war. We need to rekindle that feeling, or else we are finished. Remember, we are competing with America and even Europe for 'market share' of world Jewry, and if we can't keep our own people here, let alone attract the Diaspora to join us, then we are done with. That is why we need to change that paradigm with the Arabs, my friend."

"David, again I have to agree with Mordechai," Safran says, addressing Halevy directly, "and here the possession of Sinai will be absolutely critical for us. In this nuclear age, our seizure and holding of Sinai will give us a landmass that is four times our current geographical size. This will ensure the survival of a Jewish state after a first strike. By introducing nuclear warfare into the region, gentlemen"—Safran resumes addressing everyone—"we also have to plan for a day when such weapons may be used against us. We need to expand the size of Israel to protect our people from the huge risk we run with our current population configuration, which is all concentrated into a thin strip of land. We must disperse our people across a much wider area so they cannot be eliminated in one nuclear explosion. Given that Sinai is demilitarized as per the peace treaty with Egypt, retaking it will be easy, and hence we will spare the Egyptians another major military thrashing. Having seen us unleash our nuclear arsenal on Iran, they will be sufficiently cowed to lie down and roll over anyway."

"After all," Leiberman says, snickering, "God spoke to Moses in Sinai, so he obviously wants us to have Sinai also."

"What is key here, gentlemen," Peled stresses, "is that this is a war with no boundaries, no legal or moral inhibitions: a cataclysmic war. The Arabs have to be so wounded, so shocked, so damaged, and so cowed that they give up and *surrender unconditionally.* They need to be crushed like the Mexicans were crushed when the Americans grabbed Texas and California from them, with no hope of redress and permanently reconciled to their loss."

"Politically," Leiberman adds, "we will have a parallel strategy to deal with our friends in the West, particularly America. We will prepare a 'story' that they will be able to publicly support even if they privately harbor doubts. To begin with, our reasons for attacking Iran's nuclear sites will be understood and supported by much of US public opinion, particularly by those in the powerful and influential Christian evangelical heartland, despite the outrage that will inevitably be voiced by US liberal elites. Since the hostage crisis in 1978, Iran has been the number one demon in America's eyes, only sharing that spot with bin Laden for a little over a decade, so we won't need to worry about any public sympathy for her. When Hezbollah and Hamas retaliate on Iran's behalf, we will have a clear excuse to counterattack, this time with the publicly stated intention of putting these two 'terrorist' entities out of commission. Again US public opinion will be in our favor, and hence the Stayer administration will do little but watch and call for 'restraint.'

"Attacking the West Bank is trickier. Here we will manufacture a story that Hamas is about to take over the West Bank from the Palestinian Authority and that consequently we have no choice but to deliver a preemptive strike to prevent that from happening. Finally, and most delicate, to justify military action against our Israeli Arabs, we will claim that 'pro-Hamas imams' in mosques across Israeli Arab areas have called for jihad against the Jews in support of Hamas and Hezbollah. Since such a call will then have inevitably provoked a violent reaction from the 'right-wing extremist elements' of our society, who will attack Arab areas, the state will then be 'forced' to move into these areas for purposes of securing them and 'protecting' the minority population."

A metallic snap from Safran's lighter is followed by an exhalation of smoke, which Leiberman impatiently waves away from his face.

"Now, this 'spin' may raise eyebrows internationally," the prime minister continues, "but we will ensure that sufficient ambiguity surrounds what is really happening on the ground by interning all Israel-based foreign journalists in a hotel 'for their protection.' We will also cut all nongovernment communications out of this country, the West Bank, and Gaza, and we will heavily disrupt all communications in Jordan, Lebanon, and Egypt. Remember that our military action will all be taking place inside the fog of war, so our well-oiled *hasbara*[19] machine should be able to present our spin very effectively.

"With Egypt, we will claim that its Muslim Brotherhood-dominated government is about to intervene in Gaza, in support of Hamas. Since Hamas is a spiritual subsidiary of the Brotherhood, such a claim will not be unbelievable. This will give us the excuse to take preemptive action against Egypt and occupy Sinai.

"Finally, we will claim that in Jordan, the Hashemites, weakened and intimidated by the emerging power of populism in their country, are also about to take action against Israel in support of the Palestinians, and hence we must preempt them as well. Remember that this is exactly what King Hussein did in the 1967 war when he attacked us in support of the Egyptians. He felt then that if he didn't attack us, he would be accused of betraying the Arab cause and would inevitably face a revolution in his own country. So we have a very credible precedent here."

"Sounds like a stretch to me," Halevy responds. "You truly expect people to believe all of that?"

"Well," Leiberman answers him, "while it may stretch your credulity now as you hear it in *linear sequence*, remember that this will all be taking place in the fog of war, where we will be reacting to attacks by Hezbollah and Hamas. War is always messy, confusing, and ambiguous. We will make full use of

---

[19] *Hasbara* [Hebrew] translates as "public diplomacy in Israel" and "refers to public relations efforts to disseminate information about Israel. The term is used by the Israeli government and its supporters to describe efforts to explain government policies and promote Israel in the face of what they consider negative press (or *delegitimation*) about Israel around the world. Others view *hasbara* as a euphemism for propaganda." Wikipedia, "Public diplomacy (Israel)," last modified October 12, 2019, http://en.wikipedia.org/wiki/Public_diplomacy_(Israel).

that ambiguity and confusion to our advantage. 'Mistakes' can always be made in such a fluid, dangerous, and unpredictable environment, and trust me, we will make our share of convenient 'mistakes.' All we need is a few days, a week at most, to create situations on the ground that will be irreversible. Then historians can start the inevitable process of disputing our version, and good luck to them."

"Well, gentlemen, let's not kid ourselves," Halevy warns them, "we are obviously embarking on a project that will involve massive loss of life. Some may even see this as genocide. If that view sticks, our actions may come to be regarded by the world as a series of war crimes. As you all very well know, the UN has in place a dedicated legal infrastructure to deal with such 'crimes,' and you can be sure that after this is all over, our enemies are going to pursue us aggressively as a government and even as individuals. What are we going to do when that happens?"

"I anticipated this possibility," Leiberman answers, "and I have developed a contingency plan for it. What we will be prepared to do, if a postwar global outcry takes place, is 'reluctantly' agree to investigate all such allegations and establish an 'independent' commission with a retired chief justice of the Israeli Supreme Court to lead the 'investigation.' This commission will review all war crime allegations and eventually conclude that the government bears 'indirect responsibility' for creating conditions that allowed this to happen. While this may sound serious, in practice it means that the government will reluctantly have to accept 'censure,' basically a slap on the wrist, for excesses committed in the chaos of war, 'without our knowledge but under our watch.'

"More important, the commission will pick a prominent scapegoat if necessary, whom we can then feed to the lions. Should that happen, I plan to finger that son of a bitch Avigdor

Kahane, our 'esteemed' ex–foreign minister and coalition partner. I am sick of that arrogant prick," Leiberman spits, calling to mind the round face and tilted posture of the ex–discotheque bouncer from Moldova with whom he has had to ally himself. The prime minister is frequently disgusted by Kahane, believing that the man's provocative statements and boorish behavior, inevitably captured on film and printed in the papers, project an underlying stupidity, which reflects very poorly on Israel's global image.

"Conveniently, Kahane's party platform publicly espouses the ethnic cleansing of Arabs from Israel, and his record is littered with racist statements that can be used to implicate him. We will set him up by directly involving him in the attacks against the Arabs, which he will all too enthusiastically participate in. We will make sure that his actions in this regard are all documented so that we have a paper trail, which the court can use to fry him. The commission will consequently find Kahane directly responsible for ordering the murder and 'genocide' of the civilian Arab population and ship him off to The Hague. There he may try to implicate us, but he will have no credibility left at that point, particularly given his many other legal problems, and the commission report will have by then absolved us of any direct responsibility.

"We will have already insisted, of course, *before* agreeing to accede to the mandate of a UN War Crimes Tribunal, that it accept and incorporate the conclusions of our commission as part of its process. The UN will be so eager for us to accept their jurisdiction that they will surely agree to our conditions. Remember that the legal path to establishing any 'war crimes' tribunal is a referral from the UN Security Council, and the Americans would obviously veto such a step if we did not agree to it beforehand. So the UN will have little choice but to play ball with us."

Here, Halevy is impressed by the sheer breadth of planning for Operation King David, its architects having left little to chance.

"Obviously," Leiberman continues, "many may not swallow this story, but it will be enough for our friends in America to force the issue to be dropped. They will be able to say that while excesses obviously took place, the Israeli government has at least admitted some responsibility and arrested a former foreign minister, extraditing him to The Hague, and that taking such firm action is more than any other country has done in similar circumstances."

"What do we do if anti-Semitism breaks out in America and Europe and people there blame the Jews for the collapse of the global economy?" Halevy asks.

Leiberman signals Safran to field this question.

"That will actually be good news for us," Safran says, "since it will encourage more Diaspora Jews to come home to Israel. Remember that without anti-Semitism, Israel has little value to world Jewry. Stoking the fire of anti-Semitism in America, in order to dislodge that community from its comfortable perch and encourage those people to move here, may not be a bad idea anyway. American Jews are the last great reservoir of world Jewry. They need to eventually reside in Israel for Zionism to fulfill its mission.

"After all," he continues, "a big historic threat to Zionism has always been and remains the seductive allure of an 'American promised land' for the Jews. Today, America has been able to attract as many Jews to settle there as are living in Israel. In fact, when given a choice, Jews have unfortunately chosen to immigrate to America over Israel nearly every time. While that has obviously not meant disaster for us, since the American

Jewish community has been invaluable to securing for Israel critically needed American support over the years, even that benefit is now slowly disappearing. Today, gentlemen," Safran goes on, "the painful fact is that Israel is slowly but surely 'losing' these American Jews. America has been so good to them, and they are assimilating so well, that their affinity for Israel is gradually weakening. Our research is showing that they, particularly the younger generation, now care—and vote—much more about local American issues like taxes, government debt, and abortion than about supporting Israel. They no longer look at Israel as their refuge from another holocaust, since they cannot imagine such a thing ever happening to them in America. So their value to us as a Diaspora community will eventually evaporate, particularly as the older generation with raw memories of the Holocaust dies off."

"I can't stand these fucking American Jews anyway," Peled gripes. "They think that they can attend a lavish fundraiser with the likes of Barbra Streisand in Beverly Hills, write Israel a check for a few dollars, and then feel so proud of themselves for having done their 'duty' for Israel, while we who actually live here have to send our kids to the military, subject them to fighting the Arabs, and expose them to death."

"You are so right," Safran jumps in. "They also send their children to 'camp' in Israel to observe us like 'animals in a zoo' and then trot back to the safety and comfort of America to tell their friends all about their 'Israel experience.' Let the bastards come here and carry their fair share of the burden. We don't want their sympathy or their dollars; we want them here, on the front line, fighting with us."

"I don't know," Halevy says, grimacing, "I hope we all know what we are doing; such a huge gamble with the fate of the nation and our people! The best-laid plans can go awry! What contingency plans do we have in case things don't go the way we want them to?"

"Well, David," Leiberman reassures him, "you can look at it this way: In this war we basically have two likely endgame scenarios. The first is that the world, particularly the US, however grudgingly, accepts the new facts that we have created on the ground. Also that the Arabs, particularly the Egyptians, recognize that what they risk by continuing to resist Israel is nothing short of their very survival—and thus they capitulate, recognizing Israel as a Jewish state with her newly expanded borders. This is the more likely scenario, especially since everybody will appreciate that we have solved the Palestinian problem permanently. Now, if you think that's a stretch, David, let's look at the other scenario.

"The other scenario, a 'worst case,' if you will, is that the Arab and Muslim world erupts in anger, militarism, and terrorism; Europe and the rest of the world are up in arms against us; the US is deeply embarrassed; and the UN sanctions us. Well, David, that is pretty much a variation of what we have had to live with, on and off, for decades. The difference this time is that we will be facing these same threats from a much more powerful and fortified position. Our home front will be fully secured with the threat of an Arab fifth column's living among us eliminated; we will have borders that are much more defensible, strengthened by ample strategic territorial depth; and we will be energy self-sufficient with the oil and gas from Sinai and offshore Israel, even from offshore south Lebanon. We will also be a declared and proven nuclear power that sits on globally strategic territory astride the Suez Canal, the Mediterranean Sea, and the Red Sea with the ability to cause a lot of trouble not only for the Arabs but also for the whole world if required. If that is the downside, then this is undoubtedly a win-win strategy for Israel."

"I must say, you make a compelling argument, Prime Minister," Halevy grudgingly concedes.

"This has to be our war to end all wars," Leiberman continues, encouraged by Halevy's gradual relenting. "We will provoke international outrage anyway, so we might as well do the whole job in one blow and get it over with. The final result has to be a State of Israel that includes all of Palestine up to the Jordan River, south Lebanon up to the Litani River, and the whole of Sinai up to the Suez Canal. To succeed, we will need to move so fast and with such force that the job gets done in days, not weeks. This is absolutely essential to make sure that nobody has the time to react and organize against us. Not the Great Powers, or the Arabs and Muslims, or even global NGOs. We don't want millions of angry people in the streets of Europe demonstrating against us and pressuring their governments to react. So we will utilize surprise, maximum lethality, and speed.

"Once we launch the attack, we can have no second thoughts, doubts, or reservations until we achieve all our objectives. This will not be for the fainthearted, my friends," he emphasizes, looking them all in the eyes. "Once we are done, the Great Powers will have no choice but to accept the facts we've established on the ground. After all, who among them will be willing to fight to force us to return to the status quo ante? Even sanctions, I think, are highly unlikely, for they are imposed only on the weak, not the strong. Now, after this is all over," Leiberman concludes, "we can then settle down and worry about becoming a 'civilized' member of the international community once again, but not one minute before."

Chapter 4: Arabia Stormed

There is one source, O Athenians, of all your defeats. It is that your citizens have ceased to be soldiers.

—Demosthenes

Basra, Iraq
8 a.m., Saturday, October 8

General Javad Zarif, working from his secret headquarters in Basra in southern Iraq, receives final orders from the supreme leader in Tehran to begin the countdown to war. Basra, while nominally Iraqi, has been gradually transformed into a quasi-Iranian city over the decades. A historically important and cosmopolitan port on the Gulf, it had suffered during the Saddam years given its proximity to Iran, with war and other hostilities extinguishing its traditional role as Iraq's gateway into Iran. Today it is a bustling commercial port brimming with activity, and it is also the nerve center of Iran's very successful infiltration of the Iraqi economy. At only fifteen miles west of Iran's southernmost border with Iraq, Basra, with its thriving marketplaces, is an ideal location for Iran to distribute its goods and services, goods that have little marketability elsewhere—given sanctions and also their general low quality—since the products are manufactured in a country increasingly starved of materials, international technology, and know-how.

Accompanying Iran's economic infiltration of Iraq is a political and military infiltration that is just as effective. Militias under Iranian command have total control of the city, with Basra's central governing forces playing at best a supporting role. So it is in Basra where Zarif maintains his operational control room for the upcoming invasion, and it is here that the general sits, in an underground cement-floor bunker, surrounded by his key aides and officers, choreographing the final steps to attack.

Earlier this week, Iranian forces began their first-ever military maneuvers with the Iraqi Army on their mutual border, a border that is a stone's throw away from Kuwait. The two governments had publicly announced that they would hold maneuvers and hailed them as a sign of their cooperation and commitment to regional security. The effort was launched during an elaborate ceremony at Al Faw, the southernmost city along the two countries' shared border. Both presidents attended, each reviewing the other's guard of honor and then giving multiple speeches lauding the brotherly relations between Iran and Iraq. All this limelight, pomp, and circumstance was designed to minimize suspicion among the Americans and Arabs as to the real motives of this exercise and also to make it difficult for the Americans to object without causing the Iraqi government considerable embarrassment given the highly public nature of the event. The strategy worked; while the announcement of these maneuvers raised a few eyebrows in Washington, the Americans could see no reason to question Iraq's explanation that it was all show and little substance. The United States concluded that protesting against it would irritate the Iraqis for no substantive reason.

Yet even before the maneuvers had gotten under way, Zarif had initiated his plans to infiltrate special operations forces into Saudi Arabia, where they would play a critical role in breaching the defenses that would otherwise threaten to successfully oppose the Iranian invasion. He realized that a critical component to the invasion's success would be his ability to create enough confusion to distract Saudi security forces, opening multiple battlefronts to substantially divide their commanders' attentions and ultimately sap their strength.

His strategy was two-pronged. First, for years he had been building up "Saudi Hezbollah" as an underground Iranian-controlled guerilla movement, recruiting young Saudi Shia who came to Iran and Iraq for ostensibly innocent reasons, training them, and then sending them back to await his orders. He had also established a covert supply chain capable of infiltrating small arms and explosives to this group—all in preparation for a day just as this. Their job would be to attack Saudi military and internal security forces across the Eastern Province shortly before the invasion, diverting Saudi attention and military forces to the cities along the Gulf, even as the true threat prepared to crash through the border with Kuwait at their rear. He had also stationed political operatives among the Shia community in all major centers of Shia population in the Eastern Province, giving them instructions to begin instigating civil disobedience a few days before the invasion and to spark demonstrations— seemingly spontaneous but in fact according to a carefully orchestrated plan—that would grow increasingly violent, thereby compelling the Saudis to intervene and use force. The resultant Saudi heavy-handedness would further provoke the Shia, which would lead the Saudis to use yet more force, creating a spiraling confrontation that would culminate by the day of the invasion, also the day of Ashura, in a massive breakout of violent demonstrations that would necessitate the deployment and engagement of a substantial number of the Saudi forces available in that region. The terrorist attack in Kuwait would provide just the pretext for the Shia demonstrators to then escalate their attacks on the Saudis, breaking out their hidden stocks of Iranian-supplied weapons to open fire on the Saudis *just as* the Iranians commenced their invasion.

Meanwhile—the second prong of his strategy—Zarif's special operations units would have already infiltrated the kingdom, positioning themselves along the routes that Saudi National Guard and army units would use in responding to the Iranian invasion. Those units were tasked with both crippling the Saudi response and creating maximum chaos and confusion for the Saudis, who would already be overwhelmed with the surprise Iranian attack. This sort of planning and work was Zarif's specialty. He was, after all, regarded as the master of asymmetrical warfare in the region.

Iraqi-Saudi Arabian border
1:55 a.m., Monday, October 10

Colonel Cyrus Safavi of the Iranian Revolutionary Guard Corps steps a few yards away from his vehicle, his two bodyguards trailing at a respectful distance, and gazes south toward the berm marking the border between Iraq and Saudi Arabia, west of Kuwait. He now stands on the same ground that the Americans and their allies had crossed in 1991 as their massed mechanized forces executed the famed "left hook" that smashed the flank of the Iraqi Army. A week before, one of Safavi's trusted officers had met with a smuggler from the Ruwallah tribe who routinely operated along this part of the border. This man had been a member of a group of such Bedouin who had been very well paid over the last few months to smuggle arms and explosives into the kingdom and deliver them to Iran's agents in the Eastern Province. He was now being asked to lead the Iranian operative and his handpicked team along a smuggling route across the border and far into Saudi Arabian territory, passing north of Hafr al-Bāṭin and nearby King Khalid Military City and heading southeast, roughly parallel to the Riyadh–Hafr Highway. Safavi's officer had recorded GPS waypoints at intervals so as to mark the route, and ultimately the smuggler had died deep in the desert, his body deposited in a shallow grave hastily scratched in the sand, ensuring that he would speak to no one of this Iranian infiltration in the coming days.

Now Safavi would lead his group of hunter-killer teams—equipped with four-wheel-drive trucks, antitank missiles, mines, and the explosively formed penetrator variety of the improvised explosive device (IED) that had become so infamous in Iraq—to set ambushes along the path the Saudi Arabian Army and National Guard would take when they responded to the Iranian invasion. These ambushes would exact a price far beyond the mere killing of soldiers and destruction of vehicles. They would also magnify the inherent confusion of war as the Iranian enemy appeared far from where he was thought to be, sowing uncertainty among the Saudi commanders about where to position their forces and how best to respond, as well as engendering significant bewilderment about where the enemy might be headed. By the time the Saudi command structure could mount an effective response, it would be too late; the main Iranian force would have already reached its destination among the oil fields along the coast and be well on its way to Dhahran.

The colonel's watch beeped quietly in the darkness. It was time.

Tel Aviv, Israel
9 a.m., Monday, October 10

When compared to any other foreign power, Israel is recognized in the intelligence community as having the best human intelligence capability for monitoring Iran. A substantial community of Iranian Jews, most of whom had emigrated to Israel but some of whom had stayed behind in Tehran, supply the Mossad with qualified personnel and unparalleled connections to Iranian society. Mossad agents in Tehran had been receiving signals for some time of abnormal military activity on the Iraqi-Iranian border, including the arrival there of Iranian army units from home bases as far away as Mashhad and Tabrīz, and even from Zāhedān on the Iranian-Pakistani border, which indicated preparations that seemed to go far beyond the normal pattern of "maneuvers." As the picture begins to form at Mossad headquarters, they send a note to Leiberman, alerting him to the possibility that the Iranians are planning something other than what they had initially announced. "Not sure what, but it looks like it may be large and coordinated with the Iraqis."

Reviewing the note with Peled in Tel Aviv, Leiberman smiles: "This could be our chance; the bastards are up to something. Let's watch this space carefully and be prepared to move."

Later in the day, Israeli satellites begin picking up what they think are suspicious Iranian military formations gathering at the southern tip of Iraq, and the Mossad quickly alerts Leiberman.

Southern Iraq
5 p.m., Monday, October 10

Iran's proxy militias, the PMUs, positioned in southern Iraq in preparation for the invasion, are mobilized on Zarif's orders. Numerous but relatively lightly armed, mostly with assault rifles, light and medium machine guns, rocket-propelled grenades (RPGs), and civilian pickup trucks, their role is to follow in the footsteps of the Iranian military, taking control of Arab cities and towns as the Iranians storm through on their way to military and other strategic targets. This militia occupation force will secure the invading forces' rear while keeping the Iranian main body forces free to continue their advance. As Iraqi Shia, the men in these militias have close cultural and family ties to the Gulf Shia, which will facilitate the Iranians' efforts in connecting to and bonding with sympathizers in these communities, quickly mobilizing them to support the invasion. Also, these militias are rough and brutal, having played a key role in ethnically cleansing Baghdad and other important parts of Iraq of most of its Sunni population. They will no doubt be able to intimidate and subjugate the local Sunni population quickly. This Iraqi presence is also designed to lend the invasion a critically important "Arab flavor," framing it for presentation to the world as a joint Iraqi-Iranian operation, thereby making it more difficult for Arab rulers and the US government to cast it as being the Iranian invasion to grab Arab oil that it effectively is.

Just as important to an invasion's success as sufficient manpower and firepower are the logistics necessary to support troops and equipment. Over the past month, Zarif, ensuring that every critical detail was in place, had marshaled food, water, ammunition, fuel, spare parts, medical supplies, and more—all the myriad matériel required to wage modern war—into warehouses and innocuous-looking buildings scattered across Basra and its environs. From there, the supplies can be rapidly shuttled forward to the invasion force. This logistical component is a pedestrian but crucial piece of the attack. The Zagros Mountains, stretching across southern Iran and abutting most of its border with Iraq, are a formidable defensive barrier—a painful lesson Saddam Hussein's armies learned during the 1980–88 war—but they likewise impede offensive operations. Pushing sufficient supplies to support a large force—such as the massive formation of infantry and armor now poised on Kuwait's border—through these mountains in real time would be next to impossible. Prepositioning these supplies is the only way. Yet even with his preparations, Zarif knows he has enough to support only a few days of high-tempo offensive operations.

Still, he is confident it will suffice.

Tel Aviv, Israel
11 a.m., Tuesday, October 11

Israel has five diesel-powered submarines built in Germany to Israeli specifications, outfitted with specially enlarged torpedo tubes designed to accommodate 648-millimeter nuclear cruise missiles instead of the standard 533-millimeter torpedoes. Subsequently, these same subs were secretly fitted out at Israeli facilities with the corresponding nuclear missile capability. The submarines' armament bays carry four missiles apiece, each one armed with a 200-kilogram warhead containing 6 kilograms of plutonium. In addition, these 2,000-ton Type 800 Dolphin Class submarines, descendants of the notorious German U-Boat, are equipped with some of the most advanced sailing and combat systems in the world. They have a range of forty-five hundred miles, can remain at sea for fifty days, are able to stay submerged for three weeks, and are reputed to be the quietest subs afloat, their air-independent propulsion systems making them virtually undetectable when "invisibility" is necessary. At a submerged speed of twenty knots, they are very fast. Each costing $500 million, they form a critical component of Israel's nuclear attack deterrence systems. Equipped with nuclear-armed Popeye Turbo cruise missiles that ensure Israel a second-strike capability, these submarines allow Tel Aviv to exact the ultimate revenge if an enemy were to attack Israel with nuclear weapons. The Dolphins also extend Israel's reach with their ability to deliver missiles quickly and accurately to a relatively distant Iran. Positioned off the Strait of Hormuz, they can easily target any site in Iran and deliver their payload with only a minimum of warning.

This capability had been confirmed as early as May of 2000, when Israel carried out its first test launch of these Popeyes in the Indian Ocean off the coast of Sri Lanka, where one missile was reportedly successful in hitting a target over a thousand miles away.

While officially disclosed as being anchored at the naval base in Haifa on the Mediterranean Sea coast, three Dolphins are actually now secretly based at the Red Sea port of Eilat for the express purpose of swift and covert access to the Indian Ocean to avoid a high-profile crossing of the Suez Canal. Instructions now go out from naval command in Tel Aviv to the commanders of each submarine in Eilat to weigh anchor and move into position off the Strait of Hormuz. The cabinet is put on standby as Israeli leaders carefully watch events unfold.

Washington, DC, USA
10 a.m., Tuesday, October 11

It is late morning when CIA analysts raise the alarm. Iranian units near the Iraqi-Iranian border have broken off maneuvers and are consolidating and reorganizing into formations that—especially when combined with the massive increase in radio traffic—indicate a possible impending attack on Kuwait.

At the White House, the president's national security advisor, Tom Davis, convenes an emergency meeting of his council. "What the fuck is going on, Richard?" he barks at Richard Allen, director of the CIA, who was appointed to this potent position upon retiring from the army as a four-star general. "Where did this come from?"

A red-faced Allen responds, "Not sure, Tom. The Iranians have been in maneuvers with the Iraqis for the past week, and as you'll remember, we decided to let that pass without objection. Granted, satellite surveillance showed a hell of a lot of forces for just a 'maneuver,' especially given what the Iranians have fielded for past exercises, but our analysts were certain that it was all just thinly disguised saber-rattling intended to cow the Kuwaitis, maybe even the Saudis. The Iranians are trying to intimidate the Arabs into reducing their support for and compliance with US sanctions, yet the Saudis are leading the Arabs in the opposite direction. This is hardly the first time the Iranians have tried to bully the Arabs, so even the Saudis, whose AWACS surveillance aircraft also picked up these formations, didn't seem too concerned that it was anything more than an empty display. After all, they know as well as we do that invading Kuwait would first mean invading Iraq, and the Iraqis can't very well stand by and permit Iran to transit their territory for such a purpose—not unless they want to destroy their ties with us and end up with Iran as their only friend, that is. Yet despite this, today, suddenly, the Iranian force disposition began looking a lot more aggressive, as if they were planning to turn hostile on Kuwait. Everything we now see tells us that the Iranians are positioning for an attack, but we can't determine what their objective could be. What makes even less sense is the fact that Iraqi units remain deployed in the mix, though they are mostly toward the rear of the Iranian formations.

"I tell you, Tom," Allen adds in obvious frustration, "trying to get into the turbaned heads of these fucking mullahs is a nightmare. Why go for Kuwait? They know what happened to Saddam! Could they be that stupid? As for the Iraqis, we can't even get ahold of them. Prime Minister Mosawi is 'unavailable,' and other leaders in Baghdad are pleading ignorance and confusion." Even in tense discussion, and despite being in his early sixties, Allen retains the facial qualities of a much younger man. "We know that southern

Iraq is virtually an Iranian province anyway," he continues, "so it is even possible that the Iraqis, in all actuality, don't fully understand what is going on down there in their own backyard."

Kuwait City, Kuwait
6:16 p.m., Tuesday, October 11

As Zarif had previously explained to the supreme leader, the Iranian rulers would need to manufacture a pretext to invade Kuwait. As regrettable as it was for all of them, they decided that it would have to be a terrorist attack on a major Kuwaiti Shiite mosque. While this would obviously mean heavy casualties for their Shia brethren, the men ultimately agreed that this was a price that simply had to be paid for the greater glory of their cause. The victims, Zarif had noted in an attempt at consolation, would all certainly be rewarded for their martyrdom and go directly to heaven.

This terrorist attack and the subsequent invasion are timed to take place on the evening of Ashura, the holiest night of the Shia calendar, when the faithful commemorate the slaying fourteen hundred years ago of their revered Imam Hussein. Ashura is the day when the collective emotions and passions of the Shia reach a fever pitch. It is a time when they come together to remember and reenact scenes of Imam Hussein's murder, driving each other into a frenzy of outrage and grief.

An attack on a Shia mosque at that moment, Zarif knows, will have a devastating effect on the faithful. Covered live on TV, as surely it will be, it will ignite Shia outrage across the entire region, and they will pour by the millions into the streets, demanding retribution. Then Iran and Iraq will have the perfect excuse to move into Kuwait, to "protect" its Shia minority.

The Maghrib prayers begin at 6:16 p.m. Fourteen minutes later, at exactly 6:30 p.m., as more than three thousand Shia in Kuwait City's dome-centered, squared-off Al Abbas Mosque are entranced in passionate prayer and lamentation, a series of large firebombs explode all over the edifice. As screaming crowds trample each other in panic, trying to escape, they find all the doors have been locked from the outside, and they are quickly enveloped by a sizzling blaze of fire and explosions. Within minutes, camera crews arrive outside the mosque to film this awful scene, and it subsequently plays out live on TV. By the time Kuwaiti emergency services personnel arrive, the mosque is already consumed in flames and is rapidly burning to the ground.

It is later learned that loss of life is total.

Washington, DC, USA
10:40 a.m., Tuesday, October 11

At that moment in the White House, an aide slips a note to Davis, alerting him to the blast. Heads immediately turn to the monitor tuned to CNN, and soon enough the live pictures start to stream into the Woodshed—the nickname for the Situation Room located on the ground floor of the West Wing. All present watch in shock as the tragedy unfolds in front of their eyes. Little by little, all the while, news trickles in from other cities in the region. The monitors show the Shia erupting in fury, whole mobs going berserk and demanding revenge in the streets of Tehran, Baghdad, Manāma, Qatif, and al-Hasa.

Tehran, Iran
8 p.m., Tuesday, October 11

An hour after the horrific blast in Kuwait City, Ayatollah Motahidi appears on Iranian state television to address the "Shia of Arabia." Speaking in Arabic, a language that he, like most Iranian theologians, has mastered, he proceeds to offer his condolences to the families of the "martyrs in Kuwait" and to the "people of Islam" with regard to this heinous crime, committed on this most holy of days and therefore evidently designed to cause maximum pain and suffering for the Shia. "Such tragedy is not new to us, however," he asserts. "'Our people' are used to suffering, and it always brings us closer to God, something our enemies perpetually underestimate." He then blames the crime directly on the "kings and emirs of Arabia," who, he claims, have since the days of Imam Hussein been persecuting the Shia. "This time," he promises, his voice raised and breaking with emotion, "the Shia of Arabia are no longer alone. The Almighty, in his infinite wisdom and blessing, has decided to bring your travails to an end by way of your brothers in Iraq and Iran. Your time of liberation has come," he cries. "Prime Minister al-Mosawi and I have ordered the 'soldiers of Islam' to go forth and free you from the tyranny of the Zionists, the crusaders, and their local agents, these traitor emirs."

Tel Aviv, Israel
6:45 p.m., Tuesday, October 11

In Tel Aviv, Leiberman listens in amazement to Motahidi's speech. He immediately gives the order to summon the full Israeli cabinet for a meeting the next morning.

Baghdad, Iraq
8:15 p.m., Tuesday, October 11

Soon after the supreme leader's speech, the US ambassador in Baghdad, Jim Crocker, receives a call from Mosawi. Crocker, recently appointed to this ambassadorial position, is of the generation of US diplomats who spent many years working in Iraq (and in Washington on the Iraqi file) and who, as a result, built close personal and professional relations with many members of Iraq's Shia-dominated leadership, Mosawi among them. Crocker is thus one of many US civilian and military officials who have invested time, energy, and credibility in "preserving" the US project in Iraq and who therefore feel a special sense of ownership of it.

"Mr. Crocker," Mosawi begins, "you saw what happened tonight with this awful terrorist attack in Kuwait. The Iraqi people are going wild as you can probably hear on the street. I have concluded, with the greatest reluctance, that my government has no choice but to support the Iranians in intervening to protect the Shia of Arabia. If we don't, we will have a revolution on our hands and be thrown out of office by the angry mobs. Please understand my awkward position and be patient with us. You have my word that I will do my best to calm things down as soon as I can. Iraq needs your support; otherwise, everything the US has built with us here since 2003 will come crashing down. We are a friend to and an ally of America, and I want you to know that I have insisted, before agreeing to participate with the Iranians, on obtaining the personal assurances of Ayatollah Motahidi that US personnel, facilities, and also *wider interests* will be protected in the Gulf. This action tonight is not directed at the United States in any way. We recognize America's role in the region; however, both the Iranians and we have to take action. We cannot let such crimes continue against our people in these Sunni sheikhdoms. Please assure President Stayer of my commitment to work with the US to manage this mess as best as I can, and just please give me some time to put out these fires, before we all have an even bigger catastrophe on our hands."

Washington, DC, USA
12:30 p.m., Tuesday, October 11

Once Mosawi hangs up with him, Crocker immediately dials the White House to speak with Davis. "Look, Tom," Crocker says, "we need to appreciate that it is America, after all, that put this

Iraqi democracy in place, and now we can hardly blame Mosawi for exhibiting a democratic politician's obvious need to pander to populist outrage. Let's not overreact, and let's give him some time to work on calming not only his own people but also the Iranians. Let's see how this plays out. I trust Mosawi and know him to be a sensible, cautious guy. He wouldn't be taking this course of action if he had any other choice. All I have to do is put my head out the window and I can hear the mobs flipping out in the streets. In fact ..." Crocker opens his embassy office's window and holds the phone outside for a few seconds, giving Davis a fuller sense of the insane ruckus on al-Kindi Street just outside the compound walls. Satisfied, he shuts the window and continues. "Did you hear that, Tom? The same thing must be happening all across the region."

"But, Jesus, Jim," Davis responds, "the bastards are invading Kuwait, for Christ's sake! How can we let that stand?"

"Screw Kuwait," Crocker responds. "Why should we put the interests of a few superrich Arabs ahead of those of forty million Iraqis and eighty-three million Iranians?"

"Even so," Davis argues, "how can we let Iran storm into Arabia and give the mullahs control of all that Arab oil? We are basically letting the fox into our chicken coop!"

"Well, Tom," Crocker responds sarcastically, "hate to tell you this, but they are already in the coop. They obviously did not wait to ask us for permission. Look, Tom." He pauses, his tone changing from flippant to frank. "Let's take a step back for a moment, be realistic, and evaluate all that is happening very carefully. The picture down here has changed, and we need to recognize that. Today we have an Iraq who is a friend of America, eternally grateful to us for liberating her from Saddam. And let's not forget she is now a democracy, not some family business like the royals run in the Gulf states, and that she has nearly as much oil as the Saudis do. Also, maybe the Shia are destined to become the leaders of this region. They claim, after all, to be the majority community around the Persian Gulf. In addition, we have maybe two million Iranian Americans who connect us to the nation of Iran, and polls have continually shown that Iranian public opinion loves America. It's no longer black-and-white over here, Tom, and we all have to wake up to this new reality. Arab princes, sheikhs, and potentates are yesterday's story. They are dinosaurs that we have been propping up. Even the Iranian mullahs have a quasi democracy now. Sure, it's not perfect, but it's a hell of a lot better than some sheikhdom! So, I urge you, let's take a deep breath and revisit many of our assumptions before we rush to judgment."

"I hear you." Davis sighs. "What a mess! Let's see what the president thinks."

Iraqi-Kuwaiti border
8:30 p.m., Tuesday, October 11

Shortly after Motahidi begins his televised speech, the Ninety-Second Armored Division—Iran's premier tank formation—crashes through the Kuwaiti border at multiple points of entry, two brigades headed for Kuwait City and a third turning slightly inland, to establish a screen line between the main invasion force and the Americans who are encamped in the Kuwaiti interior. The Kuwaiti border force, whose role is to serve as a tripwire alerting its central command to any border infractions, falls back in shock. Behind the Ninety-Second Division are the Seventy-Seventh Infantry Division and three infantry divisions of the Iranian Revolutionary Guard (IRG), tasked with securing Kuwait.

This is but a single thrust of the multipronged Iranian campaign, however. A few miles east, positioned so as not to interfere with the Kuwait invasion force, are the Eighty-First, Sixteenth, and Eighty-Eighth Armored Divisions spearheading a larger force that includes five Iranian infantry and commando divisions backed by thousands more IRG soldiers and Iraqi militiamen. These units will swing west of Kuwait's populated areas in order to move more quickly and avoid interfering with the operations of the Ninety-Second and Seventy-Seventh, heading generally toward the irrigated farmland around Wafra and the Kuwaiti-Saudi border beyond it.

Two additional forces, each composed of a commando brigade and two IRG infantry divisions, are sent to secure the Kuwait Air Force bases at Ahmed al-Jaber and Ali al-Salem. The Ali al-Salem mission is particularly sensitive as the air base is not just a Kuwaiti installation but also serves as an American air base.

The Iranians know that the death of even one American service member at their hands is likely to trigger US military action, so it is their priority to avoid such an event at all costs. Fortunately for Iran, Ali al-Salem doesn't pose a threat to Iranian forces since it houses mostly training and transport aircraft and helicopters. The two Kuwaiti ground-attack squadrons aren't based here but are instead at Ahmed al-Jaber, about forty-two miles southwest of Kuwait City. Ahmed al-Jaber will thus be hit hard, fast, and mercilessly, while at Ali al-Salem the Iranians will initially content themselves with surrounding the base and occupying the runways, only later taking control of the Kuwaiti aircraft and personnel.

The US compounds at Ali al-Salem, which sit at the northeast and northwest corners of the base, are completely separate from the rest of the complex and are easily identifiable. The strategy is that small teams, each led by a senior Iranian officer, will approach each compound to announce to the American commanders that Iran has no hostile intent toward them and also that—subject to Iranian inspection of their aircraft—they will even be permitted to continue flying transports with US personnel into and out of the base once Kuwait has been secured.

Ahead of the advancing Iranian forces, missiles begin raining on key targets. A barrage of Fateh-110 short-range surface-to-surface missiles pummel Kuwaiti army, navy, and air force bases with high explosives—though Ali al-Salem is spared. Kuwaiti Patriot air defense batteries are able to intercept a few Fateh-110's, but the Iranians deliberately mass their fire to overwhelm those defenses. Some of the missiles land astray of their marks and fall among residential and commercial areas of Kuwait City and surrounding locales. Panicked civilians, many with memories of the 1990 Iraqi invasion all of a sudden revived, cram a few cherished possessions into their cars and then choke the streets and highways as they head south, interfering with the Kuwaiti military's response to the attack.

Even if it weren't for the congestion of refugee traffic, Kuwait's defenders would still not be faring well. Kuwait's army is only eleven thousand strong—a fraction of the invading force's number—and is trained and equipped for a single primary purpose: to defend in place for forty-eight to seventy-two hours until outside reinforcements arrive. Its units are structured as "cadre" units, skeletons manned at 80 percent strength and intended to be filled out by the nearly twenty-four thousand reservists that make up the remainder of the army. It takes time to mobilize reservists, however, and time is the one commodity Kuwait does not have in the face of this relentless Iranian assault. Moreover, though the hapless defenders have no way of knowing it yet, holding in place for two or three days is a pipe dream because ultimately no help is forthcoming.

The Kuwaitis push forward scores of their main battle tanks and infantry fighting vehicles. The suddenness of the Iranian invasion has found the Kuwaiti military unprepared, and in desperation the commanders deploy its powerful armored vehicles piecemeal—a platoon or two here, a company there—rather than as the massed armored fist that military doctrine intends them to be. Some fall victim to the onrushing tanks of the Iranian Ninety-Second Armored Division, but many more are destroyed at the hands of IRG tank-killer teams, both on foot and traveling in pickup trucks, which swarm the Kuwaiti tanks and employ antitank missiles and RPGs against their vulnerable, thinly armored rears.

Many of Kuwait's fleet of thirty-nine F-18 Hornets have survived the missile barrage against Ahmed al-Jaber and take to the air, intent on devastating the aggressors with conventional unguided iron bombs, cluster munitions, and air-to-surface missiles. Unfortunately for the pilots, though, the Kuwait Air Force is dependent upon US support—nonexistent at the moment, since these days US Air Force operations in the upper Gulf are minimal—to provide airborne early warning, electronic warfare, intelligence, and targeting data. The Hornet pilots find themselves fighting an air battle reminiscent of those of wars decades ago, when a pilot's eyes and his aircraft's instruments and radio were the only sources of information. The fighter pilots stalk the battlefield looking for targets, but distinguishing the friendly tanks and troops from enemy tanks and troops in the total darkness of Kuwait's northern desert, where a confused and pitched battle is raging, and furthermore with no vectors from airborne controllers, is a nearly impossible task. Some pilots are willing to risk fratricide to destroy the Iranians, in their zeal killing Kuwaitis along with—or instead of—the enemy. Other pilots are more reluctant to release weapons when unsure of their target—which is often—and in the end, the

Kuwait Air Force is unable to contribute anything substantial to defend its tiny country.

Ultimately, the most effective component of the Kuwaiti defense—and at this point its last hope—is its two dozen Apache attack helicopters. These roam the battlefield, their infrared sights easily locating vehicles in the open desert at night. Hellfire missiles make short work of Iranian T-72 and M60 tanks and BMP-2 infantry fighting vehicles; the 30-millimeter cannons and 2.75-inch rockets chew up the small pickups favored by the IRG infantry. Yet despite the excellent countermeasures on board the Apaches, enough Iranian man-portable antiaircraft missiles are launched so that some eventually find their marks. Soon, burning hulks of downed Apaches dot the open desert of northern Kuwait. Despite the effectiveness of the Apaches and the bravery of their pilots, their numbers are simply insufficient to stem the onrushing Iranian tide.

The reality is a simple one: the Iranians are able to overwhelm the Kuwaiti defenders with their vastly larger numbers. By 10 p.m., the vanguard of the Ninety-Second Armored Division reaches the Highway 80 interchange at the western tip of Kuwait Bay, just north of the Jahra suburb of Kuwait City. But because urban warfare is the main province of infantry, the trailing infantry divisions now move ahead, passing through the front lines of the Ninety-Second. Alongside the lead infantry units are trucks mounted with loudspeakers. As the Iranian forces spread through the Jahra, Waha, and Nasem suburbs, these trucks broadcast looped messages warning Kuwaiti civilians not to resist and exhorting the Shia to join their brethren in the streets.

The capture of the highway interchange triggers a key phase of the Iranian plan. Minutes after the Ninety-Second Division commander radios word of his location to higher headquarters, the rotors begin turning on rows of Iranian helicopters staged along the runway at the airport outside Ābādān, just across the border from Iraq and fewer than thirty miles southeast of Basra. Aboard are commandos outfitted with night vision goggles, submachine guns, and grenades. Thirty minutes after the helicopters lift from Ābādān, these handpicked men are rappelling down braided ropes onto the roof of Bayan Palace, where they quickly overwhelm and neutralize the armed guards posted there. Precisely placed explosives gain them access to the palace's interior in under two minutes. Here they spread out like running water, searching the chambers of the massive building for their quarry. The emir and his closest family members have already fled, but the Iranian commandos, tasked with ensuring the decapitation of the Kuwaiti government, gun down without hesitation or mercy everyone they find inside.

Those elements of the Kuwaiti army based in the country's south, now alerted, try to regroup, but at this point the initiative is indisputably with the Iranians. The Kuwaitis are all but impotent against the thousands of battle-hardened Iranians storming in, a veritable sea of sand-colored camouflage-patterned fatigues, the soldiers' passions inflamed to a raging fever by that night's terrorist attack on the mosque. Within seven hours of having crossed the Kuwaiti border, the massed Iranian armored and infantry forces reach the Saudi border. Saudi forces are surprised and overwhelmed as they desperately try to identify and intercept the multitude of enemy tanks, infantry fighting vehicles, and truck-mobile infantry units storming their border at multiple locations. It takes little effort for the Iranians to barrel through at top speed on their way to Dhahran and the oil fields.

At this juncture, the Iranian invasion force splits into two groups. One—the larger of the two—rolls southeast along the coast, generally following Highway 95 and leaving behind a force to invest Khafji, close to the Saudi-Kuwaiti border, and secure the group's rear. The other force veers nearly due south, following a course headed inland and toward Nuayriyah so that it can secure the flanks of the main effort, which is intent on taking Dhahran.

Eastern Province, Saudi Arabia
1 a.m., Wednesday, October 12

Since early October, Zarif's operatives had been very active in fomenting attacks against Saudi forces, which in turn provoked the Saudis to crack down even harder, which then incited the Shia to express their fury in various forms: demonstrating, rock throwing, tire burning, and vandalizing government property. Riyadh was subsequently forced to deploy National Guard and internal security units equipped with armored personnel carriers and armored cars into the cities of the Eastern Province. The assumption was that such a massive show of force would cow the demonstrators and get them out of the streets. The government was determined not to allow a resumption of the attempted uprisings of the past. But now, on the night of the invasion, events take a deadly turn. Instead of intimidating the protestors into relenting, the Saudi military presence in Eastern Province cities, its armored vehicles moving aggressively against the mobs, further enrages the Shia protestors. And so it is at this point in time that "Saudi Hezbollah" cells—trained, advised, equipped, and assisted by the Iranians—break out hidden stocks of RPGs and IEDs that had been smuggled in during the preceding months, and they open fire on the Saudi armor.

Powerful as they are on the battlefield, armored vehicles are exceedingly difficult to defend in urban areas. Tonight, in coordinated attacks from rooftops and alleyways, small tank-killer teams target the vulnerable, thinly fortified tops and rears of the Saudi armor. Within two hours, the burning hulks of Saudi military vehicles litter the streets of Dammam, Qatif, Saihat, Awamiyah, and al-Hasa. Panicked Saudi commanders debate whether to reinforce their beleaguered forces in these Eastern Province cities or else send more troops to the Saudi border areas to stem the onrushing Iranian tide. Confusion reigns as the Iranians take clear advantage of the Saudi dilemma and storm in.

Washington, DC, USA
5:30 p.m., Tuesday, October 11

It is now early evening in the Oval Office as a demonstrably worried president is ensconced with his national security team. He has absolutely no desire to get stuck in another war in the Middle East. He had, after all, claimed the ending of the United States' wars abroad as probably his most important achievement, and hence he has no wish to tarnish that precious legacy. A war with Iran, he knows, would redefine his presidency permanently, and most likely in a negative light. His gut instinct is to do everything possible to avoid such an outcome.

"Gentlemen," he begins, "let me start by clearly defining our national interest in the Persian Gulf in light of what is happening. We need to be clear about this before we decide to take any action and jump into this mess with all its risks. *At a minimum*, our national interest in the Persian Gulf is to ensure *the continued free flow of oil from the Gulf to world markets!* While the US with our shale oil today imports hardly any oil from the Gulf, the oil market is a global one, and any reduction in flows out of the Gulf will dramatically push up worldwide oil prices with a massive negative impact on the global economy. So that is the priority for the United States; anything else is secondary and, frankly, now irrelevant. The questions before us are: Can we still protect this national interest of ours in the Gulf, or have we lost control of the situation? Also, are we at risk of getting stuck in the middle of an Islamic civil war, a nightmare scenario if I ever saw one? What are the implications for us if we intervene to try to stop the Iranians? Can it be done, and if so, at what price?"

The CIA's Allen responds first: "The Iranians, Mr. President, have obviously surprised everybody with the audacity and brazenness of a land invasion and particularly by the fact that they somehow persuaded the Iraqis to join them. Who could have imagined that? Now, this 'terrorist attack' in Kuwait is just too convenient not to have been instigated or even carried out by the Iranians, not that that makes any difference now. In any event, it has obviously helped them achieve their objectives, which appear to be threefold: inflaming the Shia, bringing Iraq in with them, and giving them an 'excuse' to go in and defend 'their people.'

"We don't buy that story, obviously, and the Arabs certainly don't, but you know what, *US public opinion might just buy it!* No doubt, Iran has taken a huge gamble. We can be sure that they understand absolutely that it is an existential gamble for them, and hence they will throw everything they have behind it not only to ensure success but also to resist us if we intervene. So we need to be prepared to go all the way with the Iranians if we jump in. This would be total war with them, their allies in Iraq and in the Gulf, and even Hezbollah. They will turn it into a Shiite-American war with everything that might entail, including, ultimately, acts of terrorism. Now, attacking them will also probably mean we will have to massacre tens if not hundreds of thousands of them, like we had to do with the Chinese in the Korean War. And that won't even be the end of it. Remember, these guys are the animals who in the Iraq-Iran War sent their children to walk on Iraqi minefields and clear them. The monsters even gave each kid a little 'key to heaven' to tie around his neck! So we have to be prepared for doing battle with people of this mind-set and with these capabilities. We basically need the stomach to fight such a war and see it through to its conclusion, not forgetting that it will play out nonstop, in all its gory detail, on people's mobile phones in this age of new media! Let's face it: this is not Saddam's army that will crumble when the US cavalry rides in. The Iranians are a different crowd, driven by a sense of mission—a religious, 'divinely inspired' mission, if you will—and they will fight and fight hard, refusing to surrender until they are absolutely crushed. Even then, we will still certainly face an ongoing Shia armed insurgency, which is something even the Israelis couldn't handle and gave up on after nineteen years of fighting the Shia in south Lebanon—and here such an insurgency will be situated in the delicate and highly flammable heart of the world's oil industry."

"In any event," Hank Williams, the defense secretary, seated on the edge of one of the two sofas, points out, "we don't even have the troops on the ground today to stop these guys. We only have a few thousand personnel in Kuwait, and that includes a lot of support staff. Thus far, the Iranians are leaving our bases in the Kuwaiti interior strictly alone, although our reconnaissance shows that they've deployed armored forces along a screen line east of the camps. We've got prepositioned equipment stocks there, enough for two heavy brigades, but it would take days to prep that equipment for combat, to say nothing of providing the logistical support needed to sustain those units in a prolonged fight. With the Kuwaiti and Saudi ports in the hands of the Iranians, we'd be reduced to bringing in fuel, ammunition, spare parts, and literally every other resource by air or through a port on the Red Sea, both of which are difficult and time-consuming options. The bottom line is that our presence today in the Persian Gulf is built around the navy and air force, with a minimal complement of ground troops, mainly for force protection. Airpower alone certainly won't stop these Iranians. We estimate that they will very quickly have over a hundred and fifty thousand men, among their regular troops, the IRG, and the Iraqi militias, spreading like ants all over Kuwait and—we have to assume—on their way to Saudi Arabia and likely even Bahrain, with still more troops poised to pour in behind them. Plus, they are organized into small and highly mobile units. This is a lot more sophisticated than an old-fashioned armored invasion with tanks and heavy equipment."

Williams pauses for a few moments to have a drink of water. The atmosphere in the Oval Office is heavy with tension. Others in the room take this opportunity to digest the information.

"Iran seems to be pursuing a dual strategy, going for strategic oil facilities and also rushing to embed her forces in local population clusters. While the Saudis have spent billions upgrading their oil infrastructure security, thanks in part to our assistance, it has all been designed to interdict a terrorist or missile attack, not to repel an all-out assault by a professional army. Frankly, Mr. President, if the Iranians continue south into Saudi Arabia, we expect them to slice through the Arabs like a hot knife through butter and be all over the Eastern Province of Saudi in hours.

"To stop them, we will have to go in and take them on, man-to-man. At the end of the day, the only way to root out the enemy from an area you don't want totally destroyed, such as a friendly city or an oil field, is with infantry moving from building to building—and even by following that strategy, the destruction will be considerable." The secretary stands, walks beyond the carpet to the parquet flooring, and looks out of the twelve-foot windows directly behind the president's desk. "By the time we mobilize to do that, they will have embedded themselves within supportive local Shia communities. A frigging human shield if I ever saw one! Confronting their forces will also surely involve the killing of thousands of civilians, and you can be certain that they will torch every Saudi and Kuwaiti oil facility in the interim. A vicious war to liberate eastern Arabia is guaranteed to put its oil industry out of commission for years. That's 25 percent of global oil production, gentlemen," he says, turning around to face the others, gauging the impact of this last statement. "But an oil price increase will be the least of our problems. With that amount of oil out of the market, who knows what will happen to the global economy. Let's not kid ourselves," the secretary concludes, walking back to the sofas, "the Iranians are a bull that just burst into the china shop. We can eventually take him out, but you can then kiss that china shop goodbye, for a good while at least. Frankly, I think these bastards truly have us by the balls, Mr. President," he says, looking directly at Stayer, whose hands are clasped tensely before him on his desk. "At least that's the view from Defense at the moment."

"I agree with Hank," adds Davis from one of the chairs in front of the fireplace. "Also, let's not forget another factor that should impact the way we look at the whole question of Persian Gulf oil going forward: *America is actually self-sufficient in energy!* Foreign oil is irrelevant to us now. So let us bear this fact in mind, gentlemen, before we consider committing our boys to war again. In any event, for now at least it seems that we have little choice and may just have to accept the reality of Iranian control over Arab oil and work with it. Mosawi has made it very clear to Ambassador Crocker that the Iranians will respect our 'interests.' Their oil minister is now being quoted on the wires as saying that the Islamic Republic is fully cognizant of its responsibility to ensure the safe and secure delivery of *all* Persian Gulf oil to global markets with only a minimum of disruption. So they are making the right noises. At the end of the day, they ultimately need to sell all that oil. They can hardly drink it! Granted, we would obviously very much prefer not to have an Iranian hegemon in control of 50 percent of the world's oil reserves. That is hardly an ideal scenario. Preventing one strong party, or even two, from controlling the Persian Gulf and its oil has been the basis of British policy and subsequent US policy for over a century. But what is the choice we now have, and how costly is the alternative? Also, with Iraq involved, we need to think long and hard before we act rashly and destroy everything that we've painstakingly built over there—and at a huge cost, I might add. Mosawi and the Iraqis could potentially serve as a very useful intermediary between us and the Iranians going forward, so let's not burn any bridges with Iraq now by acting impetuously. We are on the ground in the Gulf, after all, and the Iranians will have a great incentive to cooperate with us. They will probably bend over backwards to accommodate us in the beginning to make sure that we accept this new reality, and they will know that we will retain the capacity to take military action in the future if they don't play ball. Given these factors, I say we wait and see what happens."

"Well, that sounds like a sensible recommendation," the president responds. "Let's take some time and think this through. For now, let's just put our forces on alert and call for a UN Security Council meeting. You can announce that to the press, Tom, so we at least show some kind of action on our part."

The president then prepares to receive the Treasury secretary and the chairman of the Federal Reserve, both of whom have been waiting impatiently, glued to their iPhones, outside the Oval Office. Once signaled, the two men rush in, an aura of high anxiety surrounding them. "Mr. President," the secretary blurts out, "financial markets are imploding; the Dow has already dropped by 10 percent and will surely continue plummeting tomorrow. Overseas markets when they open will no doubt follow. Gold has crossed the twenty-five-hundred-dollar mark and is rising, and oil futures are at two hundred dollars and also rising fast. Now this was all the initial knee-jerk market reaction in the few hours before closing. We believe that markets, once they have fully absorbed the impact of developments in the Gulf, and particularly if the Iranians invade Saudi Arabia, will freak out even more. They will assume the worst: basically that Saudi and other Arabian Gulf oil production will cease for the foreseeable future. The European markets are already very shaky and vulnerable, and China and Japan's financial markets, with economies addicted to Persian Gulf oil, are surely going to crash the minute they open in the morning. Our banks are obviously heavily exposed to all these markets and are already facing liquidity problems. The Fed has consequently been aggressively pumping money into the system, trying to preserve investor sanity and order. Frankly, Mr. President, we need to make sure that any action the United States now takes in the Gulf *helps calm things rather than exacerbate them.* Otherwise we may end up staring a global economic collapse in the face."

Dhahran, Saudi Arabia
3:15 a.m., Wednesday, October 12

At Aramco "City," the town-sized headquarters compound of Saudi Aramco, the national oil company, details start to come in to its security command center of unidentified groups of vehicles heading toward them.

As would be expected of the world's largest oil company, the custodian of the greatest concentration of oil reserves on earth, Aramco has at its disposal a world-class security infrastructure. This infrastructure had also been strengthened with an updated antimissile and antidrone umbrella. The one problem with the design and implementation of these security measures, however, is that the force was equipped and trained to protect the oil infrastructure *from terrorism and airborne attacks but not from an armed invasion.* This latter is a very different adversarial situation to prepare for.

In creating this security infrastructure, the foremost priority was that it protect the Saudi oil infrastructure against just these types of threats. And accomplishing such an objective was no small feat: the infrastructure is enormous with thousands of miles of exposed pipelines, storage facilities, and oil rigs at sea and in the desert—all vulnerable, all highly flammable, and all terribly exposed.

It is also notable that lately the Saudis have felt increasingly less secure behind the US security umbrella. Before, they hardly worried about an invasion via their northern border since everybody agreed the Iranians would never be that adventurous. By 2005, al-Qaeda's terrorism had reached Saudi Arabia; as a result, the government's security focus logically shifted inward so as to deal with this threat. Then in 2015, a major war broke out on the Saudi-Yemeni border, requiring military intervention and a massive relocation of men, equipment, and other resources to the kingdom's southern border. The culmination of all these factors is that today, in October of 20XX, the Saudi army's attentions are focused on maintaining security elsewhere, and hence tonight, the forces manning the Eastern Province— primarily the National Guard and internal security troops—are geared more toward maintaining internal control than repelling a foreign army.

Given the reports already flowing out of Kuwait over the past few hours of an Iranian invasion force, there is little question among the security command as to who the interlopers are en route to breach Aramco. Those in the command center immediately contact their superiors in Riyadh with the grim news, and then they declare an alert across all Aramco facilities.

King Abdul Aziz Air Base, Dhahran, Saudi Arabia
3:30 a.m., Wednesday, October 12

As Aramco's head of security begins passing instructions to the company's many installations, his words are interrupted by a series of ominous, thundering booms from the south. Concussive waves knock framed pictures from the walls and small objects off of shelves, and everyone in the room can feel the vibration through the soles of their feet. This reverberation is the effect of Iranian Shahab-2 short-range ballistic missiles, each carrying a seventeen-hundred-pound payload of high explosives, falling one after another on and around the Saudi Air Force base only a couple of miles away. Two squadrons of F-15 fighters, along with three squadrons of Tornado ground-attack aircraft also based there, are mostly parked under shelters along the flight line. Even near-misses from the massive Shahab-2 warheads wreak havoc upon the fleet. Coupled with the missiles' range of over three hundred miles is the fact that most of them retain substantial quantities of unexpended fuel upon impact. The resulting widespread fireballs only add to the carnage.

The Saudis' US-built Patriot surface-to-air missile batteries near the Gulf engage as the first Shahab-2's come within range. These Patriots are the newest variants, far superior to the ones employed with mixed results against Iraqi SCUDs during Desert Storm, and each battery's radar system is capable of tracking a hundred different targets simultaneously. However, that same radar can guide no more than nine missiles at a time, so the Iranians have launched a massive barrage specifically intended to overwhelm Saudi antimissile defenses. Many Shahab-2's are intercepted, but not enough. Within thirty minutes, nearly 50 percent of the combat aircraft at King Abdul Aziz are damaged, but also, more important to the Iranians' strategy, the runways there are rendered useless. Meanwhile, massive fires light the skyline of the surrounding city.

Fortunately for Saudi Arabia, a good chunk of its combat airpower is located on bases far away in Riyadh and Tabuk, as well as at Khamis Mushait on the southeastern side of the Arabian

Peninsula. The Iranians, abreast of this intelligence, launch a few dozen of their precious Shahab-3 and Ghadr medium-range ballistic missiles—capable of throwing a 1,760-pound warhead well over a thousand miles—at the King Faisal and King Fahd air bases in Tabuk and Taif, respectively. Most slip past the Saudi Patriot batteries, which are busy engaging the lower-altitude Shahabs raining on Dhahran. Despite this, the Iranians know they will still have to suffer some punishment at the hands of Saudi fighter pilots, at least until their forces are embedded in the cities of the Eastern Province, but now at least there are fewer aircraft to mete out that punishment.

Riyadh, Saudi Arabia
3:45 a.m., Wednesday, October 12

In the royal palace, Saudi king Mashari, still awake after learning news of Iran's attacks, receives an urgent phone call from his chief of staff, Khalid al-Otaibi, informing him that the Iranians have crossed the Saudi border. The king is already apprised of the terrorist attack on the Kuwaiti mosque and the subsequent Iranian-Iraqi invasion of Kuwait, but early information coming out of the country remains confusing and unclear. Moreover, the king had been trying without success to contact the emir of Kuwait, so he remains somewhat in the dark.

Mashari is indeed shocked by Otaibi's report that the Iranians have dared to attack his kingdom, as well as by the fact that they have been able to move so quickly. He, like many other observers when they first heard the news, had initially thought the Iranians and Iraqis would only target Kuwait and that the Saudi kingdom would at least have some time to mobilize itself and its friends.

"We are mobilizing our forces, but many of our units are either along the border with Yemen or else engaged with protestors in the Eastern Province," Otaibi explains gravely. "The air bases at Dhahran, Tabuk, and Taif have all been hit by Iranian ballistic missiles within the last half hour, and Dhahran in particular lost many aircraft, but we will be blasting the Iranians with every bit of ordnance on board every fighter plane available. The Iranians are moving along the coast right now, however, so I can only assume they are headed directly for the oil fields—and at the moment there is little in their path to stop them." He finishes and awaits the king's answer.

"Gather my advisors and the general staff. We will meet within two hours, and at that time I want to know everything they know," the king directs Otaibi.

King Fahd Causeway
4:30 a.m., Wednesday, October 12

Even as Iranian troops are marching relentlessly toward Saffaniyah on the coast, an elite commando force is about to storm the Saudi–Bahrain causeway to secure it. Spanning sixteen miles, this causeway is one of the longest bridges in the world. Construction was completed in 1986, thereby creating a land bridge between Saudi Arabia and its tiny and vulnerable ally Bahrain. With a landmass over two thousand times smaller than Saudi Arabia's, and easterly situated a bit south of the midway point of Saudi Arabia's eastern shore, Bahrain, an island until then completely isolated in the Persian Gulf, was previously a sitting duckling for either an internal revolution by its majority Shia population or an Iranian invasion—or both. A key objective in building the causeway was to give Saudi troops quick wheeled and marching access to Bahrain should military assistance to Bahrain's ruling family be required. And, in fact, this very situation had presented itself in 2011, when the Saudi military came into the diminutive kingdom at the behest of the Bahraini government to help quash an uprising by Bahraini Shia.

Today, however, the Iranians are determined to make use of the causeway for the exact opposite reason. They would be incapable of reaching Bahrain by following a seaborne course, the traditional route for any Iranian invasion, because the United States' massive resources at the US Navy's 188,000-square-foot Bahrain base would surely notice and easily squash their efforts. Such a seaborne attack is exactly what the US military infrastructure in the Gulf is designed to deal with, and hence Iranian forces would hardly be able to leave their ports before being identified, tracked, and probably destroyed. Now, however, the Iranians are slipping in through the back door, a totally unexpected point of entry, with plans of mounting a simple, low-tech variation of invasion from the sea, which neither the Bahrainis nor the Americans are mobilized for or able to stop. This assault will turn the causeway intended to be Bahrain's salvation into the instrument of its downfall.

A rusty, nondescript freighter chugs through the dark waters north of the causeway, gliding to a stop as the engines slow to an idle. Crew quickly lower Zodiac boats over the sides, and Iranian commandos clamber down cargo nets into the boats, each small craft moving away to circle slowly in the darkness as yet more Zodiacs are loaded. Once the entire assault force is staged, the boats turn their bows southward and throttle up, setting out for the small island near the midpoint of the bridge that holds the customs stations and checkpoints in charge of regulating the Saudi-Bahraini border.

The immediate objective is not only to provide a means for the invasion force to enter Bahrain but also to connect the Shiite population of Bahrain with that of eastern Saudi Arabia as quickly as possible. This area is the heart of "Shia Arabia," and reconnecting the two parts of that community is a critically important step in sustaining their collective enthusiasm for the invasion. It is not even necessary for Iranian forces to reach the capital city of Manāma before mobs take matters into their own hands and start burning down the Al Khalifa palaces there—action that is prompted by strategically placed Iranian operatives.

The lightly armed forces that man the Saudi-Bahraini border— tired and at the nadir of human attentiveness given the early hour—are no match for the Iranian commando force, and they are slain before they can muster any appreciable resistance. Teams pour across the causeway in both directions, securing the Saudi and Bahraini ends of the bridge to await linkup from Khobar on the Saudi mainland once the Iranian main body reaches them. Meanwhile, the decrepit freighter pulls alongside the quay on the north side of the midchannel island, unloading more Iranian troops and heavy weapons. Man-portable antiaircraft missiles are deployed in the event Saudi or Bahraini helicopters attempt to insert troops for a counterattack, and antitank missiles are dug in to defeat tanks or armored cars, but no such threat is forthcoming from the Bahraini end of the causeway. Bahrain's mercenary army of Pakistani, Syrian, and Jordanian troops, having heard that the Iranians were coming and soon thereafter learning that the causeway had fallen, has no interest in attempting to retake the bridge and therefore simply melts away at the mere rumor of these angry hordes.

Saffaniyah, Saudi Arabia
5 a.m., Wednesday, October 12

Within half an hour of the Iranian vanguard's crossing of the Kuwaiti-Saudi border southwest of Wafra, the surviving elements of the Royal Saudi Air Force begin pounding the invaders with every bit of airborne ordnance available. Hellfire air-to-surface missiles seek out tanks, infantry fighting vehicles, and armored personnel carriers, their impacts sending turrets and gouts of flame flying into the air, followed by lingering pillars of black smoke. Cluster munitions scattered in the path of the advancing invaders destroy trucks and shred dismounted infantry. Smart bombs dig massive craters into roadways.

Yet for all the high explosives unleashed in defense of the kingdom, the Saudi pilots are failing to stop the advancing tide. The common tactic for employing airpower against ground forces, *interdiction*—impeding the movement of enemy forces by severing key links in the transportation network, for example, by destroying bridges or obliterating roads at choke points—is simply not a viable option here in the open desert. Unfortunately for the defenders, the land along the shore of the Persian Gulf is flat, wide-open terrain. Damaging the few highways in the area doesn't bring wheeled troops to a halt because military vehicles and four-wheel-drive trucks alike simply continue traveling across the sands. The Iranians are able to advance across such a broad front in the areas where no inviting concentrations of vehicles present themselves. Saudi aircraft are reduced to picking off individual fast-moving vehicles, a relatively simple proposition with guided missiles but no mean task with bombs, and in any event a laborious process akin to dismantling a sandcastle a pinch at a time. Also, each aircraft carries only a limited loadout of munitions and must return to base for rearmament before rejoining the attack. Worse yet, the stock of guided missiles stored at those bases is hardly an unlimited supply. Precious minutes burn away as the Saudi fighter-bombers rotate to and from the battlefield—minutes during which the Iranians press forward, heading southeast along the coast at breakneck speed toward the Saudi oil fields.

Two hours after having crossed over into Saudi Arabia, the Iranian vanguard reaches the oil production facilities at Saffaniyah, about sixty miles from Kuwait. Detaching a small force to secure the area, the main body then continues south, veering well away from the multiple pipelines that traverse the desert, those parallel steel channels carrying the lifeblood of the Saudi—and the global—economy. The Iranians are not interested in the sprawling desert sands of Saudi Arabia; their concern is for the oil wealth that lies beneath them. The more collateral damage the oil infrastructure suffers, the longer it will take to restore production, and the more likely it becomes that other nations will intervene. Understandably, then, Iranian commanders are under strict orders to minimize damage to the oil fields.

The Saudi pilots pursue the vanguard south, chiseling slowly away at, and with a growing sense of futility in the face of, the Persian legions.

Manāma, Bahrain
5:15 a.m., Wednesday, October 12

At the royal palace in Bahrain, the king urgently contacts the US admiral of the Fifth Fleet, stationed at the naval base on his island, asking for help. The admiral quickly explains to the king that his capability on the ground does not exceed force protection—that is, ensuring the security of the base, the naval port, and all associated US personnel—and hence there is nothing practical he can do to be of assistance. He does, however, grant the king and his family and key government officials permission to flee immediately to the protection of the base and escape the roaring mobs headed toward their palaces, an invitation that the king quickly accepts. Al Khalifa issues instructions to his large family, spread across the island, to head to the base immediately. Within twenty minutes' time, the king and his key aides, ducking to avoid the spinning rotors, board a helicopter. It lifts off, setting out for the safety of the US naval base.

Camp Sayliyah, Qatar
5:30 a.m., Wednesday, October 12

At US Central Command at Al Udeid in Qatar, confusion reigns. With no standing orders on how to handle a land invasion of Kuwait, the military brass are at a tense standstill, awaiting instructions from Washington. Other than ensuring that all US forces in the Gulf are put on high alert, there is little they can do until the White House makes decisions and issues directives.

Riyadh, Saudi Arabia
5:50 a.m., Wednesday, October 12

While waiting for his advisors to assemble for the meeting, King Mashari calls his ambassador in Washington, Adel Shahrani, to find out how the Americans are reacting. Shahrani, spending a late night at the embassy on New Hampshire Avenue, reports that the Americans are being evasive and inaccessible, and notes also that he senses general confusion at the White House. "The American economy," Shahrani tells the king, "is already in a recession, and the administration is panicking, afraid that this crisis could push their economy into a meltdown. As a result, the economic aspect of the crisis seems to be their immediate priority." Shahrani promises to report back to his monarch as soon as he can get any clarity from the White House.

The king's national security team gathers in his office. Mashari sits at his imposing desk, senior princes and generals spread out in front of him. "The Iranians," General al-Mulla, his land forces commander, tells him, "have already reached Saffaniyah and are well on their way to Jubail. In Qatif, Saihat, and Dammam, and even in Khobar, our security forces are still fighting with protestors and armed elements who will obviously join up with the Iranians once they arrive. I say 'when' rather than 'if' because while our airpower has been able to draw blood from the Iranians, it has been overwhelmed by their numbers, and hence it does not seem that airpower will succeed in stopping them. We are sending forces from King Khalid Military City in the north to engage the Iranians, who have established a defensive line here"—Mulla gestures at a large map behind himself—"and we hope they can make an impact. The only good news—and I can barely call it that—comes from Aramco security," he continues. "They report that there has been minimal damage to the oil facilities captured by the Iranians thus far—it seems the Iranians are being quite deliberate about that."

"No doubt," the king replies with a frown. "The Persians are not here to 'rescue' our Shia, no matter what Motahidi declares to the world. Rather, they are here to grab our oil." He pauses, considering, and the men in the room with him remain respectfully silent, allowing him time to pick up speaking again. "What are our remaining options to stop them?"

"Nobody expected or planned for an Iranian force advancing via a ground route through Iraq," General al-Mulla responds. "Even the Americans have been taken completely by surprise. Our military was simply not mobilized or prepared to deal with such an attack, so our resistance is patchy and disorganized. Also our police, National Guard, and military are taking hits from all sides by regular and irregular Iranian troops and even local pro-Iranian agents. We've suffered hundreds of casualties and lost dozens of armored vehicles to ambushes and attacks by protestors in all the major cities of the Eastern Province."

The king has never trusted the Iranians, despite their many publicized efforts to reach out to him, so he is actually not overly surprised that they have taken action against his kingdom—although the brazenness of the attack does shock him. He has always felt in his bones that this Persian Republic would prove to be the ultimate existential threat both to his kingdom and the existing order in Arabia, but he had expected the Iranians to take a more asymmetrical approach—for example, by arming pro-Iranian elements of the Saudi Shia minority and directing them to carry out acts of sabotage and terrorism—rather than orchestrate something as bold as a full-blown invasion. Mashari had frequently conveyed to the Americans his concern about Iran's imperial ambitions, famously quoted in the WikiLeaks-exposed State Department cables as telling senior US officials that they needed to "cut off the head of the snake" before it was too late. The United States' tepid response to his warnings, however, had made him worry about the onset of US fatigue regarding war in the Middle East and the United States' gradually weakening will to take on the Iranians despite the US government's private and public protestations to the contrary. While the United States had announced after its withdrawal from Iraq in 2011 a new security "arrangement" for the Gulf, designed to reassure the Saudi king and other Gulf leaders, Mashari knew that it wouldn't be "arrangements" but rather the political will to fight—the willingness to put, as the Americans had phrased it, their "men and women in harm's way"—that would keep the Iranians at bay.

Mashari turns to his aides seated close to him. "I spoke earlier to Shahrani. The Americans are confused and also distracted by the economic impact of all this, so it seems unlikely they will do anything quickly. We are on our own for now," he tells them. Realizing that the Iranians are probably no more than three hours away from Riyadh by highway, he asks about preparations for the defense of the capital and is informed that all available forces are now mobilizing to protect it.

His head of security, Colonel al-Malik, comes in just then and advises him that the leadership should take no chances by staying in Riyadh, particularly given what he has just learned: that an Iranian helicopter-borne commando operation went directly for the Kuwaiti leadership. The colonel suggests that the government members immediately relocate to Jeddah, on the Red Sea coast. He informs the king that he has already ordered a plane to be readied and now requests that they all move without further delay. The king agrees, and the men are transported in a heavily guarded convoy directly to Riyadh Air Base, where they board waiting aircraft.

Saudi airspace
7:15 a.m., Wednesday, October 12

In his private Boeing 747 with his key aides, in the air on their way to Jeddah, where they will land and then be taken by car to Mecca, the king raises the idea of calling on the Pakistanis for help. "Today, Pakistan is the only power that has the capacity to come to our aid against the Iranians, if the Americans are unwilling to," he offers.

"Yes," responds his foreign minister, who was among those convoyed to the plane, "but asking Pakistan to attack Iran, which is a country with which she shares a long border, is no easy request to make."

"I realize that," the king responds, "but frankly it may be the only hope we have. The Pakistanis owe us a lot, and on top of that they stand to *lose* a lot if the Iranians take over Arabia. An Iran with such enhanced power should scare them half to death since any new Persian empire will inevitably try to intimidate Pakistan into becoming a client state. I am confident that the Pakistanis will give serious consideration to my request." The Saudi royals and others present continue to discuss the many facets and implications of enlisting Pakistan's help until the airplane begins its descent. Once on the ground, the king deplanes and is escorted into one of a fleet of armored cars that were awaiting his arrival. Then Mashari and his entourage speed by road toward Mecca, Islam's holiest city, reaching their destination thirty minutes later.

The royal palace in Mecca, a massive, heavily fortified concrete structure, had been specially built to give its residents unobstructed views of Islam's holiest shrine, the black, cube-shaped Kaaba. It is usually in this palace that the king receives and hosts foreign Islamic leaders who have come to Mecca for their annual pilgrimage, the hajj, but today is different; the atmosphere is tense with a hyperalert Royal Guard on edge as the king makes his way to the door. Even in Mecca, a sacred city to Muslim Arabs and Iranians alike, the Saudis can never be sure that the Iranians have not planned a terrorist attack to accompany their invasion.

Jubail, Saudi Arabia
7:20 a.m., Wednesday, October 12

The Saudi land forces, on whose collective shoulders the defense of the kingdom now principally rests, are faring little better than the air force. Many of their heaviest units remain deployed too far south, along the Saudi-Yemeni border. And many other Saudi troops, along with heavy units of the National Guard and internal security, are now embroiled in the cities of the Eastern Province, much of their heavy equipment already burned-out hunks destroyed at the hands of Iranian-supplied protestors. The infantry forces are struggling to contain the raging mobs that have flooded the streets.

In addition to the Saudi army brigades deployed near Yemen, based mostly at King Faisal Military City near Khamis Mushait and at Sharurah, another substantial portion of ground forces is at King Abdul Aziz Military City outside Tabuk, near the Gulf of Aqaba and the Jordanian border. All are too far away to intervene in time. Those units that are available to respond to the invasion are the Eighth and Twentieth Mechanized Brigades found at King Khalid Military City, or KKMC, which was built in the 1970s and '80s in conjunction with the US Army Corps of Engineers and was later used by the Americans during the Gulf War. It is located approximately one hundred fifty miles southwest of where the Iranians crossed into Saudi Arabia.

The troops, tanks, and infantry fighting vehicles of the Eighth and Twentieth Brigades—the remaining sole hope for the kingdom's defense—pour out of their base in ragged columns, preparing to head across the open desert to the east. But the Iranians have laced the routes away from KKMC with mines and deadly explosively formed penetrator IEDs, so before they ever see their enemy, the Saudis begin taking casualties. Shocked commanders halt their formations, calling forward engineers to clear the routes before any further movement is undertaken. The clearing process is painstaking and time-consuming; precious time is lost before the Saudis begin marching again.

Iranian unmanned aerial vehicles are monitoring their progress, however, and the infiltrated hunter-killer teams—another demoralizing obstacle—are positioned along the route that the Saudis must take to reach the invasion force. There the Iranians wait with more mines and IEDs, along with antitank missiles and three-man teams armed with RPGs ready to pop up from spider holes. The combat that takes place once the Saudis reach these positions is sudden, sharp, and brutal, culminating in the Saudis' favor. The open desert offers few opportunities for ambushers to withdraw and thereby live to fight another day, and the Iranian force ultimately dies almost to the man. Nevertheless, it has accomplished its objective. The Saudis are consequently delayed, disorganized, and weakened, by now having lost nearly half their heavy vehicles.

Yet, with those infiltrators defeated, the Saudis now face the southern axis of the Iranian invasion, the one that had previously turned south and headed for Nuayriyah. This force is responsible for screening the flank of the main effort of the invasion, and thanks to the multiple delays the Saudis have suffered, it has had time to begin digging into defensive positions. Military doctrine calls for a minimum three-to-one local superiority for an attacking force to succeed against a defender, and the Saudis are unable to consolidate their remaining forces enough to muster a credible threat to the more numerous Iranians. This Iranian line holds, and behind it the Iranian vanguard rolls south out of Saffaniyah.

It takes less than two and a half hours for the Iranians to cover the next hundred miles to Jubail, which is little more than a company town for the Saudi Basic Industries Corporation, the kingdom's petrochemical giant. Saudi security forces offer what resistance they can, but as the battalions of Iranian special forces detailed to secure Jubail arrive, they storm in without hesitation, using indiscriminate force against any moving target. What little resistance the lightly armed Saudi security forces can muster amounts to no more than a brief impediment to the Iranians.

Once it is clear that the Jubail-detailed force will require no assistance to accomplish its mission, the Iranian corps commander orders his forces south again. Dhahran—and beyond it the King Fahd Causeway that leads to Bahrain—is less than sixty miles away.

Dhahran, Saudi Arabia
9 a.m., Wednesday, October 12

The Iranians continue to surge south, detaching a battalion to secure King Fahd International Airport while the vanguard turns east to swing south of Dammam. As the invasion force approaches Dhahran, the headquarters of Saudi Aramco, the lead tanks crush fences and gates and topple barriers as if they were toys. Groups of heavy vehicles turn north and south to complete the encirclement of the complex, while IRG commandos stream in and begin taking control of the city. Though sporadic house-to-house and building-to-building combat will continue for some hours more, it is impossible to deny the outcome: Iran has overrun the heart of the massive Saudi oil industry.

To the east, dozens of tendrils of smoke rise into the morning sky from Bahrain. One brigade of the invasion force has pushed forward to the Saudi end of the King Fahd Causeway for a victorious linkup with the commandos who have been holding the bridge. Meanwhile, the remaining Saudi resistance melts away.

Gulf region
12 noon, Wednesday, October 12

By noontime the next day in the Gulf, which is 4 a.m. at the US capital, about sixteen hours after breaking through the Kuwaiti border, the Iranians are crawling all over Kuwait and eastern Saudi Arabia and are now moving into Bahrain.

In Kuwait, the emir and those senior members of his government who were able to do so have fled; others are in hiding; and the least fortunate, caught by the invaders, are dead. The Kuwaiti military has collapsed with most of the air force having withdrawn to Saudi airfields. Kuwait's army is dispossessed, its armored vehicles having been appropriated by the Iraqi militiamen tasked with occupying the small country, and its small arms having been distributed to the invading forces' allies among the Shia population. Every member of the Kuwaiti officer corps that could be found is under arrest. Some ten thousand Iraqi militiamen and another forty thousand Iranian regulars and IRG soldiers now control Kuwait. The US forces based in the interior are heavily armed and on a war footing, and they have dispatched armored vehicles and additional forces to Ali al-Salem to secure the American airhead there, but so far neither the Americans nor the Iranians have made a hostile move toward the other.

The southern shore of the Persian Gulf from Kuwait to Bahrain— and with it the bulk of the Saudi oil industry—is virtually under Iranian control. Damage to the facilities has thus far been minimal. Because of the Saudi ground forces' failure to breach the screen line and reach the main body of the invasion force, along with the Saudi pilots' reticence to mount attacks near the installations, the stern Iranian directive to protect the oil fields has been successfully carried out. Pro-Iranian Shia mobs throughout the Eastern Province have been armed and are now being organized into neighborhood militias to maintain control. Saudi military forces have withdrawn along a line crossing the Riyadh–Dammam Highway. Tiny Bahrain is in the hands of pro-Iranian elements.

Roughly two hundred thousand Iranian and Iraqi soldiers and irregulars are now dispersed among the populations and infrastructure of three Persian Gulf nations, two of which are entirely in the hands of the attackers and their local supporters, save for the fitful resistance of scattered holdouts.

In Iran, the ninety-thousand-strong Basij militia has mobilized its three hundred thousand reservists. While those forces are being deployed predominantly to maintain internal order and border security in the absence of most of Iran's ground forces, Iran has also begun mobilizing the reserve component of its regular military—something it could not do until the invasion commenced. Since the mobilization of reservists is a clear prelude to war, intelligence agencies would have certainly detected it, which would have nipped the Iranian offensive in the bud. Within days, Iran will have another eight hundred thousand men available to stream into the conquered territories, should the need arise.

Iran is by now well on the way to acquiring direct control of over 25 percent of the world's oil production capacity and will soon raise that figure to 30 percent when it inevitably takes over the UAE and its supposed "friend" Qatar.

Mecca, Saudi Arabia
12:30 p.m., Wednesday, October 12

By noon it had become crystal clear to King Mashari, who had been deliberating with his closest advisors for four hours about the wisest and most effective course of action, that if there was to be any US intervention on Saudi Arabia's behalf, it would not come in time to stop the Iranians. So Mashari concludes that it is time to call on the Pakistanis.

Saudi Arabia's remaining hope against an Iranian takeover is no doubt Pakistan, which has been called, albeit with some exaggeration, an army with a country rather than a country with an army, in recognition of the fact that the Pakistani military effectively rules the nation. While a facade of democracy has mostly been observed, mainly to satisfy the United States and other Western allies and donors, key decisions are now made—as they have always been made—by the generals. Historically the generals have quickly disposed of any politician who tried to tamper with the formula, so Pakistan's current president, having no illusions about his proper place in the structure of real power, wisely satisfies himself with the perks and prestige of the presidential office, staying out of the generals' way.

Since its establishment in 1947 as an independent state for the Muslims of India, Pakistan had naturally felt a close affinity with Saudi Arabia given the kingdom's status as the birthplace of Islam and host to its holiest sites. The Saudis, in turn, had reciprocated this affection and developed a special sense of responsibility to support Pakistan over the years.

This relationship also included very close Saudi military ties with Pakistan. In the early days of the relationship, there were even Pakistani combat units stationed on the ground at key border locations across the kingdom. But that arrangement had begun to dissolve after Operation Desert Storm, with the United States' arrival on the scene. Now cooperation is focused more on training, joint intelligence work—particularly in Afghanistan— and continuing Saudi financial support of Pakistan's military.

Included in this military aid is support for Pakistan's nuclear program. Such a program was and continues to be a hugely expensive undertaking for a country with limited financial resources, so when the Pakistanis turned to the Saudis in the 1980s, seeking financial assistance for this program, the Saudis gladly obliged, realizing that a Pakistan-based nuclear arsenal, the development of which they had supported, might one day come in particularly handy for their own security purposes. Saudi leaders consequently feel today that it is a realistic choice for King Mashari to make such a monumental request of Pakistan's generals.

Sitting behind his desk, the king instructs his assistant to place the call. Rather than asking to speak with the Pakistani president, however, whom the king does not like or trust, he instead contacts the Pakistani army chief of staff and strongman General Ashfaq Afzal directly.

"General," the king begins, "I call you from a Mecca that is now under threat of Iranian invaders. Iranian missiles have fallen on Saudi cities. Iranian troops are seizing the cities of the Eastern Province one after another. The Americans have let us down, and now we have only our brothers in Pakistan to save us from this menace. You have nuclear weapons that can cripple these people, and at this stage nothing else will stop their advance. We are all at the mercy of a Persian monster who wants to dominate Arabia and Islam, and if this monster is not stopped, *all of us* face destruction. Only Pakistan and a quick decision now by Your Excellency can save the Holy Land from these deviant aggressors."

"Your Majesty," Afzal responds, "we are absolutely shocked by this news and very worried about you and our brothers in the kingdom and the Gulf. I am relieved to hear you are safe. You can be sure we will not let you down. Pakistan was created to serve Islam, and you honor us with your request. I will consult with my government and get back to you as soon as I can."

After General Afzal hangs up with King Mashari, he immediately calls a face-to-face meeting of his army corps commanders, who, along with Afzal and the army's head of intelligence, are the de facto rulers of Pakistan. Such a sensitive discussion, he determines, can hardly be had over the phone. The commanders, spread all over the three-hundred-thousand-square-mile country, will need until the next day to finally assemble together in Rāwalpindi, near the capital city of Islamabad. In the meantime, Afzal instructs his staff to study and prepare for him and the other generals a full review of the situation and of Pakistan's military options.

Chapter 5: Israel Pounces

The expulsion of the Palestinians [by the Israelis] would require only a few brigades. They would not drag people out of their houses but use heavy artillery to drive them out; the damage caused to Jenin would look like a pinprick in comparison.[20]

—Martin van Creveld, professor of military history, Hebrew University

Jerusalem, Israel
11:30 a.m., Wednesday, October 12

The full thirty-member Israeli cabinet convenes at the Cabinet Office in Jerusalem. Prime Minister Leiberman addresses those present. "Gentlemen," he begins, "as you know, last night the Iranians, with Iraqi support, invaded eastern Arabia. They seem to be attempting a takeover of the whole Persian Gulf region, and so far they are well into occupying the entire eastern oil-producing rim of Arabia down to and including Bahrain. The Americans and the Arabs are in total shock, having been

---

[20] Martin van Creveld, "Sharon's Plan Is to Drive Palestinians across the Jordan," *The Telegraph,* April 28, 2002, accessed November 11, 2011, http://www.telegraph.co.uk/news/worldnews/middleeast/israel/1392485/Sharons-plan-is-to-drive-Palestinians-across-the-Jordan.html.

taken completely by surprise. We, however, were not caught entirely off guard since Mossad alerted me a few days ago that something was cooking on that border. The Iranians have taken a terrific gamble, and at this stage it's difficult to predict how it will play out. Everything will depend on the Americans and how they react, and Washington is still trying to absorb the facts and understand the implications. We cannot see much that the Americans can do at this stage, unless they are willing to destroy Iran completely.

"For us, however, this development is supremely convenient. It is a regional and global political and military earthquake that provides us with the ideal conditions to launch Operation King David. And, with a world already shocked by their invasion, we have all the more reason to hit Iran.

"Consequently, I would ask the cabinet to approve the immediate launch of our submarine-based nuclear missiles against six key Iranian nuclear sites. We will not target anything else, so as not to disrupt the continued Iranian invasion of Arabia. Indeed, let them cause havoc and continue to distract the whole world. We do expect Hezbollah to retaliate, but if they don't, we will claim a Hezbollah rocket attack and move in anyway; but let's hope that they do shoot at us, as that would give us easy political cover. Ideally a similar situation will develop with Hamas in Gaza, and then we'll go out with all guns blazing.

"Gentlemen, this is the most important decision any Israeli cabinet will have had to make since the first cabinet decided to proclaim the establishment of the State of Israel in 1948. We are about to embark on a war that will ensure our survival, in perpetuity, as a Jewish state. We need to stay strong and united as this unfolds. We should expect a lot of noise, not only domestically from the left but also from the world community. We have to be willing to bear this pressure, stay focused on our mission, and entertain no second thoughts or doubts. Once we start, we cannot stop until we achieve all of our objectives."

After a short debate focusing primarily on how to manage the Americans, the cabinet votes with a solid majority in favor of the prime minister's proposal.

Gulf of Oman
4:30 p.m., Wednesday, October 12

Deep in the Gulf of Oman, off the Strait of Hormuz, two Israeli submarines receive their encrypted instructions. The mission commander is Vice Admiral Haim Rothberg, a thirty-three-year veteran of the Israeli Navy and one of the architects of its submarine warfare strategy. Given the importance of this mission, he has been assigned to command the Dolphins and tasked with final authority on launching the missiles. Rothberg is highly cognizant of the historic import of what he is about to do, and in fact he had read extensively beforehand about Paul Tibbets, the US pilot of *Enola Gay*, the B-29 Superfortress that dropped "Little Boy"—the first of two atomic bombs used against Japan toward the end of World War II—on Hiroshima. He wonders how history will remember him for pushing the button that began this era's nuclear war, but at the same time he has no doubt that this is the right course of action for Israel. Once Rothberg reads the decoded message, consisting of one simple word, *David*, he passes the directive to the submarine captain, who orders his crew to battle stations and begins the countdown to launch. On board the other Dolphin, keeping station three and a quarter nautical miles from Rothberg's position, similar preparations get under way.

Within minutes, six nuclear-tipped Popeye Turbo cruise missiles are fired at their respective targets: the processing facility at Natanz; the light-water reactor at Būshehr; the

Parchin military base, eighteen miles from Tehran, which is the center for Iran's nuclear weapons development; the heavy-water reactor at Arak; the research and yellowcake uranium processing site at Esfahan; and the underground uranium enrichment facility at Fordow, just north of Qom. Each submarine retains one missile ready to receive targeting data and mount a follow-up strike in case any Popeye Turbo in the first wave fails to reach its target.

At the Būshehr nuclear power plant it is late afternoon. Staff are all at their stations busy at work when the missile hits, creating a fireball that incinerates the whole facility and all personnel within a mile of the resulting crater. The missile launches have been carefully timed so that all six strikes will occur within a two-minute window, and as it happens the other five missiles reach their targets over the next fifty seconds. The outcome at four of the sites is similar to that at Būshehr, but at Fordow, a more recently constructed facility deep within a mountain, the impact is different. While all aboveground infrastructure is destroyed, the people inside the plant and bunkers, more than ninety feet below ground, survive but are effectively buried alive. They will not, however, live for long. All downward-reaching access points are destroyed, as are power, communication, water, and air feeds. These workers and researchers are all suddenly entombed deep within the earth's crust, and only limited oxygen remains. Given that heavy earthmoving equipment would have to be transported to the site, given the time it would take to dig through nearly a hundred feet of dirt, rock, and concrete—some of it fused into a solid mass by the heat of the nuclear blast—and given the radioactive contamination of the entire area, all factors that would seriously impede rescue efforts, there is no chance of digging into the mountain and reaching the people trapped there in time to save them.

Washington, DC, USA
7:30 a.m., Wednesday, October 12

In the Oval Office of the White House, the president is engrossed in his morning briefings when Tom Davis bursts into the room. Stayer looks up anxiously, knowing that the news Davis is bringing is unlikely to be good. "You aren't going to believe this, Mr. President, but the Israelis have just taken out six Iranian nuclear facilities with their own submarine-launched nuclear missiles."

"Jesus!" exclaims the president, jumping to his feet. "Get everybody in my office immediately."

Tehran, Iran
6 p.m., Wednesday, October 12

The supreme leader is in his quarters when alerted that he has a call from General Rowhani. "Your Excellency, our nuclear sites have been hit with what our people believe to be nuclear weapons. We are not sure who is behind this, but it's probably the Israelis."

"Let us meet immediately in the command bunker," the leader answers. He then leaves his quarters under heavy guard and is rushed to a helicopter, which stands ready to transport him to a nuclear shelter built deep into a mountain on the outskirts of Tehran, where he will join his military commanders now awaiting his arrival.

While Motahidi is in the air, the Israeli prime minister's office releases a statement. It confirms that Israel has carried out nuclear missile attacks on six Iranian nuclear sites. Israel, the statement explains, had publicly warned the international community, repeatedly for decades, about the Iranian nuclear threat. Today, with Iran's hostile intent and subsequent threat to regional peace and stability nakedly exposed, the government of Israel felt that it could no longer wait and, in so doing, allow the Islamic Republic to secure nuclear weapons capability. Because the State of Israel could not eliminate the Iranian nuclear threat by using the conventional military forces and tactics at its disposal, and since the international community was unwilling to carry out its responsibility to help Israel in this regard, the Israeli cabinet reluctantly concluded that they had no choice but to utilize nuclear weapons in order to neutralize the Iranian threat. Included in the statement is a declaration that Israel will take no additional military action against Iran beyond the destruction of these facilities. The world, the statement concludes, is a safer place today as a result of Israel's actions.

Tehran, Iran
6:20 p.m., Wednesday, October 12

Ten minutes after takeoff, the supreme leader's chopper touches down at the heliport outside the bunker, and he is swiftly escorted inside to the large conference room. Waiting there are Defense Minister Rowhani, National Security Advisor Jalili, and other key military commanders and intelligence officers. Those present immediately inform Motahidi of the Israeli statement, and they all sit down to discuss it. "What is your assessment?" he asks them.

Rowhani responds first: "Sir, they have obviously damaged our nuclear program very badly. These capabilities are difficult to re-create quickly. We still have some satellite facilities dedicated to working on our nuclear program that are spread around the country, but those that were hit are the main sites. More important at this stage, however, is the message the Israelis are sending us, which is that they will attack with nuclear weapons before they ever allow us to develop our own nuclear weapons capability. So that is something we will have to bear in mind."

"What about the fallout from the nuclear explosions?" Motahidi asks.

"The Israeli missiles detonated as airbursts, sir, so the fallout will have limited impact beyond the sites themselves," Rowhani answers him. "Also, the warheads for such missiles would have had to be relatively small, so we don't anticipate much in terms of civilian casualties beyond the targeted area."

"Good. But what about the reactor at Būshehr?" Motahidi continues. "Would that not have produced large-scale fallout such as what resulted in Japan after the accident in their reactor a number of years ago?"

"No, it would not, Your Excellency," Rowhani responds, "since the nuclear material in the Būshehr reactor would have been vaporized by the explosion—so, again, any fallout will be limited to the direct surroundings."

Jalili jumps into the discussion. "None of this is ideal news, obviously, but we can at least be grateful that the fallout won't be catastrophic. Let me refocus our attention on our objectives, however. For our purposes today, we will not be stopped by this attack. The Israelis, as per their statement, will launch no further attacks against us. So our best course of action now is to instruct Hezbollah and Hamas to retaliate. This will actually be helpful because the breakout of an Arab-Israeli war at this point will only add to America's confusion and problems, which may decrease the likelihood that she attacks us. What concerns us now is that this action has not and will not disrupt Operation Imam Hussein, and that is what counts."

"I agree with you," the leader responds. "We are now well on the way to controlling Bahrain, Kuwait, and the Saudi Eastern Province. Let us focus today on consolidating our position and bringing in more troops and equipment, and then we'll see how things develop." He concludes by congratulating everybody around the table on their success so far. The men all acknowledge the supreme leader's praise with broad, gratified smiles on their faces.

Beirut, Lebanon
8 p.m., Wednesday, October 12

An enclave called Dahiye in Beirut's southern suburbs is nearly exclusively populated by Shia immigrants from south Lebanon, and Hezbollah has turned this area into its own version of a tightly gated community. Hezbollah's leadership convenes in their bunker here, deep underground. Having already lived through a virtual carpet-bombing of this neighborhood in the 2006 war, they have since rebuilt their infrastructure, particularly this reinforced subterranean facility, to withstand virtually anything the Israelis could hurl at them short of a nuclear device. Upon hearing of Israel's attack on their Iranian patron, they knew that they would soon be asked to retaliate, and sure enough, the official request came within the hour from Iran's ambassador in Lebanon, asking for an audience with Hezbollah's secretary-general Sayed Hassan Nasrallah. The ambassador, a senior officer in the Revolutionary Guard, is Iran's official liaison to Hezbollah and is in constant contact with its leadership.

Now congregating in their meeting room, the "politburo" of the organization sit down to make the urgent decision on how to move forward. "Gentlemen," Nasrallah, his round face bordered by a black turban, begins, "as expected, our brothers in Iran have called upon us to initiate a massive retaliation operation against the Israelis, and they will be asking Hamas to do the same. I don't see that we have much choice here but to honor this request, although we all know that our organization and our people will be forced by the Israelis to pay a very heavy price for our actions. The ambassador also made an important point, namely that the distraction element of this attack is as important as the retaliation itself. The Islamic Republic is well on its way to taking over the whole Persian Gulf and destroying the existing political order in Arabia, so anything that distracts the Americans and delays their possible attack on Iran is critical to ensuring the success of the Iranian offensive. As you all appreciate, Iran is battling in Arabia on behalf of all of us, and if she succeeds, as she surely will with the blessing of the Almighty, she will dominate the Arab and Muslim world. Here in Lebanon, this will have an enormous, positive effect on our position, so every effort and resource we have must be mobilized to guarantee Iran's success."

"We should then go all out and hit the Israelis with everything in our arsenal," responds Sheikh Naeem Qasem, deputy secretary-general of Hezbollah. An older, graver, and lower-profile figure than the charismatic and telegenic leader of Hezbollah, Qasem is the ideologue of the group, a deep thinker and intellectual who takes a back seat to his boss in public but who plays a very influential role within the inner circles of the group.

"Yes, absolutely," agrees Nasrallah, "and let us quickly start evacuating civilians from the south and also from here in Dahiye so as to minimize casualties from the inevitable retaliation. We can be sure the Israelis will level this neighborhood once again—we should expect no less from them—but with Iran in control of Arabia, our standing, indeed our whole future, in Lebanon and the Arab world will change. We will be easily compensated for everything lost."

Within an hour of this meeting, at approximately 9 p.m. Beirut time, Hezbollah commences to launch a massive series of rocket attacks on sites all across Israel. Air-raid sirens scream across the country as Hezbollah's missiles, dramatically improved in range and accuracy since the 2006 war, cause considerable damage and casualties, even as far away as Tel Aviv.

Tel Aviv, Israel
9:30 p.m., Wednesday, October 12

In Tel Aviv's Hakirya District, and located beneath the Defense Ministry compound—called the Kirya, Israel's equivalent of the US Pentagon—is the underground national military command center referred to as the Bor. Huddled here with his commanders, Mordechai Peled receives the news of Hezbollah's attacks with satisfaction. "Now we can begin." He grins to his officers. "Let's move." He gives the order, and Israel proceeds to explode outward against its enemies.

This time, unlike in 2006, Israel has no inhibitions to bother itself with, given its leaders' decision to fly in the face of world public opinion, as the Israel Defense Forces (IDF) unleash a massive attack across the whole of south Lebanon. Here Israel pursues a scorched-earth policy, which Hezbollah is neither expecting nor prepared for.

A master at guerilla warfare, Hezbollah has been anticipating and training for an essential replay of the 2006 war with the Israelis—perhaps an even more intense battle than the last one, but nonetheless a war wherein the Israelis will have to navigate around civilian areas, ever mindful of world public opinion. Its members are therefore confident that their irregular methods will trump the more conventional tactics of Israel since Israel must navigate not only the actual but also the political terrain with more prudence.

Hezbollah is quickly shocked to discover, however, that the current strategy unfolding before them radically differs from the one Israel pursued in 2006. Today, Israel is simply draining the sea that Hezbollah swims in. Liberated from their former concerns and constraints, the Israelis approach this task Sherman[21] style, beginning the process of flattening the whole of south Lebanon up to the Litani River.

Israeli helicopter-borne commandos are inserted along the south side of the Litani River, seizing bridges and establishing a cordon to block any movement—of Hezbollah reinforcements and civilians alike—southward. The only traffic the Israelis will suffer the crossing of the river will be those civilians fleeing north. Meanwhile, Israeli ground-attack aircraft are dispatched to hunt down Hezbollah surface-to-surface missile launchers, while in the north the Iron Dome antimissile systems are working hard to protect Israeli cities.

With the area sealed off, the IDF begins the complete sterilization of Southern Lebanon. The first step toward this goal is the aerial bombing of major population centers, combined with naval bombardment of cities along the coast, such as Naqoura, Rachidiye, and Tyre, and artillery bombardment of those inland. The towns erupt into a series of huge fireballs, in scenes reminiscent of those beheld in the wake of the Allied firebombing of Tokyo and Dresden during World War II. Leadership targets in Dahiye and Baalbeck are attacked as well in order to disrupt Hezbollah's command and control.

These tactics bring swift results: the civilian population begins fleeing north, choking roads and creating chaos. Behind them,

---

[21] General William T. Sherman was a US Civil War Union Army commander who pursued a strategy of total warfare with intentional disregard for civilian and collateral damage as a matter of policy.

the aerial and artillery bombardment slowly creeps northward, pushing the terrified refugees ever farther ahead.

Behind the bombardment, Israeli ground forces advance. Fighting without any restraint against the use of indiscriminate force, the IDF is relying heavily on firepower. Bunkers and tunnel complex entrances are identified, lased with target designators, and destroyed with laser-guided artillery rounds or missiles. Bunker complexes are blanketed with napalm, the resulting superheated air sucking the oxygen from underground fortifications. If in the slightest doubt about the nature of a structure, the advancing soldiers call for an air or artillery strike, or one precisely placed round from a Merkava main battle tank.

Hezbollah is overwhelmed. This is not the battle they had prepared for, and the only effective answer would be for them to meet the IDF in a conventional fight—a challenge completely beyond their capabilities. Many of Hezbollah's troops are buried alive, incinerated, or suffocated in the underground fortifications that had otherwise long been their salvation. The roads are choked with hordes of civilians stampeding north, desperate for help. With Hezbollah headquarters in Dahiye and the Bekaa Valley under heavy attack by Israeli airpower, the organization's command and control structure quickly degrades amid panic, confusion, and discord.

Washington, DC, USA
4 p.m., Wednesday, October 12

President Stayer is ensconced with Tom Davis in the Oval Office, reviewing the news coming in from the Middle East. The Iranians are all over eastern Arabia, the Israelis have hit Iran with nuclear weapons, and now Iran's proxies are firing back at Israel. "The shit is really hitting the fan," he says, groaning.

"Any bright ideas, Tom?" A staffer brings in a pot of coffee and two cups, and Stayer, tapping a pack of cigarettes against his knee, considers violating his promise to the American public to observe the White House's no-smoking policy.

"Not really at this stage, Mr. President," Davis responds, stirring sugar into his cup then resting the spoon on a saucer. "There's nothing we can do except call for restraint and see how things develop. Israel's nuclear attack on Iran has further inflamed global financial markets. In fact, the Asian markets have already plummeted in light of yesterday's events, and when they open in a few hours, they'll go into complete meltdown. Gold and oil prices will continue to shoot up, and stock markets will collapse further. Maybe you should give Leiberman a call and ask for Israel's restraint, and also remind him of the global economic impact of what he has done." The president motions an aide to get Leiberman on the phone.

The relationship between Stayer and Leiberman remains a cold one, and neither of them pretends otherwise. Leiberman much prefers his buddies in the American right wing, particularly the Republican Party leaders and the evangelical "Christian Zionists," and he is at the same time convinced that Stayer is no great fan of Israel. Stayer, in turn, is irritated to no end by Leiberman's habit of constantly bypassing him and getting what he wants from a supportive Congress. "Benjamin," the president begins, "your use of nuclear weapons on Iran has elevated this crisis to a whole different level, the ramifications of which, particularly on the global markets and overall economy, will be huge. Now is not the time to debate these actions, but I do need to ask, in the name of the United States, that you exercise restraint going forward. Pouring more fuel on the fire may bring down the whole global economy, and you don't want Israel—or your government for that matter—to be held responsible for such a huge catastrophe."

"Mr. President," Leiberman responds formally and coldly, "we hardly started this. The Iranians attacked *your* allies in the Gulf. We realize, as we have been warning all along, that Iran is finally going rogue, and we suspect that America hasn't the will to stop her. We have been crying out for help with the Iranian nuclear issue for decades, and my government was simply not going to allow our people to live under the threat of a nuclear holocaust courtesy of the Islamic regime in Tehran. You knew that such an attack by Israel on Iran was inevitable; after all, we have been saying as much for years. With these crazy mullahs breaking out, we could no longer take chances or wait anymore. We decided to move against them immediately, and frankly the US and the rest of the world owe us a debt of gratitude for taking care of this problem.

"Now Hezbollah has retaliated against us, and other attacks are sure to follow. Things are moving very quickly over here, and we are in neither the mood nor the position to take any more chances with our enemies. You know that the Iranians possess advanced chemical warfare capabilities. None of us can, with any certainty, eliminate the possibility that they have transferred such capabilities to Hezbollah or Hamas. And, since we did hit Iran with nuclear weapons, we have to assume the worst when predicting their response. So today, we in Israel must behave as if we are under threat of an attack replete with weapons of mass destruction. You can be sure that we will do all it takes to defend and protect our people in front of such a risk. America's concern about the global economy is appreciated, but you also have to appreciate that we may be fighting here for our very survival, so you'll understand if global economic concerns are not at the top of our priority list."

Stayer can see that he is not going to gain any ground with Leiberman in this discussion, so he concludes by asking the prime minister to stay in touch with him and try, as much as possible, to exercise restraint. He then puts the phone's receiver back on its cradle.

Gaza, Palestine
1 a.m., Thursday, October 13

As battles rage in south Lebanon, Hamas leader Ismail Haniya and the rest of the leadership meet in their own bunker in Gaza to discuss Iran's request. Hamas, having been cut off for many years from material Arab support thanks to heavy US pressure on the Arabs, had gladly accepted Iranian help instead. While not unaware of Iran's cynical motives here as the Shia power supporting a Sunni fundamentalist organization, the Hamas leaders believed they had little choice. Unlike Hezbollah, which has open borders to Syria and beyond, Hamas is boxed in by Israel, which controls all of Gaza's air, sea, and ground borders, leaving them with only one border outlet, which is under Egyptian control. Consequently, Hamas had mastered the art of tunneling beneath the border that Gaza shares with Egypt, and its members then used these tunnels to smuggle the arms and supplies that the Iranians provided them with, again via smuggling routes that went out across the Sinai desert.

Since past Egyptian governments had been doing Israel's bidding by also squeezing Hamas, the organization formerly had nobody to turn to but the Iranians. This situation, however, had changed dramatically in Hamas's favor with the resumption of power by a Muslim Brotherhood–dominated government. The newer Egyptian government, strongly supported by public opinion, decided to remove its blockade of Gaza. As a result, Egypt had automatically replaced Iran as Hamas's most important and influential ally, leading to a commensurate reduction in Iran's influence over the organization. Still, the Hamas leadership sought to maintain its ties to Iran. With few friends in this world,

Hamas wanted to be careful not to burn the few bridges it did have, particularly now that it seemed Iran was in ascendancy in the Gulf.

After debating the issue for some time, the Hamas leadership concludes that they can hardly refuse Iran's request outright. At the same time, they have neither the desire nor the ability to withstand another Israeli military onslaught the likes of Operation Cast Lead, which had destroyed wide swaths of Gaza in 2009, or Operation Pillar of Defense in 2012, which inflicted further damage on Gaza and during which one of Hamas's key leaders was killed. Because of this, they agree that their best option is to mount a symbolic attack—launch a few missiles at a couple of targets, issue a strong statement that they are retaliating against the Israelis—but do no more than this, and meanwhile hope that the Israelis focus on their northern enemy Hezbollah and do not retaliate too severely against Hamas. "Let's do as little as we can, both to avoid alienating the Iranians and also to try to minimize the inevitable Israeli retaliation."

Having at last reached a consensus, the leadership issues instructions for the immediate launch of a limited number of Qassam rockets at the southern Israeli town of Sderot. Little do they appreciate that they have fallen into the same trap as Hezbollah; they have just provided the Israelis with the casus belli they need to begin their planned attack.

Tel Aviv, Israel
2 a.m., Thursday, October 13

Peled, still stationed inside the Bor, receives word that Hamas missiles have hit Sderot, and in turn he authorizes phase two of Operation King David.

The high population density of Gaza is of great advantage to the Israelis as it will allow them to inflict tremendous damage and loss of life very quickly. With its blockade of Gaza over the previous years, Israel had successfully prevented the import of cement and steel into the Strip; hence, today, Gaza does not have adequate infrastructure to shelter its civilians. The leaders of Hamas are among the very few with adequate protection, secured in some of the only reinforced bunkers in Gaza, which are situated below the main hospitals.

Upon receiving Peled's command to launch phase two, and in coordination with the strikes on Southern Lebanon, the IDF responds to the Hamas attack on Sderot with a ferocious artillery barrage directed at Gaza City and all population centers in the Strip. Already apprised of Hamas's bunker locations, Israel directs air attacks to level those hospitals to the ground, not only to destroy civilian morale—by exhibiting Israel's willingness this time to operate without any boundaries and hence strike terror in people's hearts, inciting them to escape while they still can—but also to prevent the Hamas leadership from surviving. The IDF then opens all the gates into Sinai to allow survivors to flee into the desert and head off to Egypt.

While the carnage in Southern Lebanon produced by the sudden Israeli air attacks on unprepared towns is horrendous, in Gaza the effects of intensive and unrelenting artillery bombardment on a large population densely packed into flimsy structures in a small, highly urbanized area are nothing short of apocalyptic. Tens of thousands of Palestinians stream through the barriers into Sinai, but they are coming from the areas not yet under bombardment. Few survivors emerge from those locations that were laid to waste.

The Israeli artillery is methodical, and as the barrage advances southwest from Gaza to Nuseirat toward Khan Yunes, IDF soldiers follow in its wake, ensuring that no one remains. The refugees spread panic as they flee for Rafah, and by the time Israeli artillery rounds and rockets fall on Nuseirat, it is mostly just empty buildings they destroy. The border crossings are clogged with traffic, and soon desperate Palestinians will have commandeered trucks to push down the border fences in several locations.

West Bank, Palestine
8 a.m., Thursday, October 13

By this time, the Israeli media are already broadcasting horrific scenes of the destruction in Lebanon and Gaza, sending a clear message to all of Israel's neighbors of Israeli tactics. By early morning, the IDF moves into the next stage of Operation King David and unleashes an artillery barrage across the whole West Bank, employing a tactic perfected in the Lebanon War of 2006 and used with brutal efficiency this morning in Lebanon and Gaza—its artillery pushing people out of their towns with what artillerymen call a *creeping barrage*, a tactic that slowly advances a continuous front of impacting rounds. High explosives rain down as Israeli unmanned aerial vehicles circle the battlefield to aid in fire control, for here—unlike in Gaza—Israeli settlements are mixed in with Palestinian towns. Though the death and destruction are not quite as wholesale as in Gaza, due to more selective targeting, Palestinians begin fleeing the artillery nonetheless. IDF soldiers posted along the Israeli border turn back those who are foolish or desperate enough to head west, leaving them no choice but to brave the bombardment for a second time in making their way to Jordan.

Word has also been quietly passed from the Israeli government to various right-wing groups—many with members who have settled in the West Bank—that the area is to be entirely cleansed of Palestinians. As the bombardment moves east, fanatic and well-armed Jewish settlers, requiring little encouragement to assist in the cleansing plan, run loose, terrorizing the Palestinians, further impelling the mass exodus of survivors to Jordan.

A false story is then leaked to Israeli television's Channel 2, alleging that "pro-Hamas imams" in mosques across Israeli Arab areas are calling from the minarets for "a jihad against the Jews." Other news outlets pick up the story, and as it spreads all over the media, it soon becomes the pretext for the all-out attack on any Arabs inside the borders of Israel.

Special units of Israeli troops in civilian clothing then begin attacking Israeli Arab towns and neighborhoods in order to intimidate the populace and encourage their flight. At the same time, groups of zealots associated with the ultra-right-wing parties of Israel, and affiliated Russian criminal gangs, are sent to assault the Arabs and to loot and plunder their properties across the Arab neighborhoods of Jaffa, Haifa, and Galilee. In the midst of all of this widespread, indiscriminate, and lawless violence, a diminishing but still lethal barrage of Hezbollah's missiles rain down, air-raid sirens blare, and general mayhem and confusion reign across the country.

Israeli police and paramilitary units are then dispatched to the Arab areas, calling on all Israeli Arabs to congregate at specific meeting points so that they may be taken into "protective custody" against the marauding bands of zealots and other gangs. These messages are repeated on the radio and television, the government imploring its Arab citizens to seek refuge within the arms of the state and protect themselves and their families from hostile gangs, which the government describes as "out of control." The announcements bring the desired effect: Arabs rush to the designated meeting points. There they find large holding areas that had just recently been quickly set up and are now manned by the Israeli police and its Civil Guard, which has also been mobilized for this operation. At each staging area, hundreds of buses and trucks idle in parallel rows, the vehicles commandeered from the public transit system, the military, and commercial trucking and transportation companies. The Arabs are herded into them in a smoothly choreographed operation, and soon the first loads—the vehicles flanked by military escorts for the supposed secure transport to safe shelters— roll away from the staging points. These convoys, however, proceed to travel at high speed to the Jordanian border, where the passengers, under the threat of gunfire, are unloaded and herded over into Jordan. Elite Israeli forces had, by then, finished taking over all entry points into Jordan, and now they throw these entryways open so that the Palestinians may flood in.

Israel has nearly two million Arabs to expel from within its existing borders, and this is not counting the four million Palestinians in the West Bank and Gaza who are already fleeing in terror of Israeli firepower. The IDF has pressed into service some twenty-five thousand buses and a few thousand trucks, capable of moving that number of people and more in a couple of trips—but naturally, the process of gathering Arabs at the meeting points, identifying and organizing them, loading them onto transport, and then unloading them at the border is far from a simple one. Nevertheless, within twelve hours every Israeli Arab who reported to a staging point will be deported, and the police will go neighborhood by neighborhood to find those who stayed behind and forcibly remove them.

Amman, Jordan
9 a.m., Thursday, October 13

It is just as the working day begins in Amman when the Israeli Air Force launches a series of air raids that hit and completely destroy the headquarters of Jordan's powerful General

Intelligence Directorate, which is the heart of the regime's police state apparatus and the ultimate symbol of Hashemite state authority. Follow-on air attacks, combined with Israeli surface-to-surface missile strikes, level the army headquarters and decimate key military bases and royal palaces across Jordan. Cratering munitions destroy the runways at Jordanian airfields, grounding Jordan's air force. The two major army installations in the east, at Irbid and outside Amman, which could pose an immediate threat to Israel, are pounded mercilessly, and later strikes hit other bases at Zarqa and Mafraq in the east and Maan and Aqaba in the south. Over the next few hours, every major military and internal security facility is reduced to rubble. Israeli planes also attack primarily "East Jordanian"[22] towns like Karak, Saalt, and Irbid with the objective of distracting what remains of the Jordanian military with anxiety about their homes and families, turning their attention away from the impending influx of Palestinians.

Meanwhile, IDF ground units push across the border a few miles into Jordanian territory. There they establish a defensive line to create a buffer zone in the event that Jordan's army attempts to move against Israel—highly unlikely, given the wholesale destruction of its command and control networks—and to ensure that the newly displaced Israeli Arabs and West Bank Palestinians move into Jordan's interior rather than cluster near the border, holding out hope of returning to their homes. The IDF's orders are to permanently demolish any illusions a Palestinian may harbor about ever coming back home to Israel.

The Jordanian leadership are so overwhelmed with shock that they crumple with incomprehension. As his palace comes

---

[22] The British created Jordan in 1921 from an area of southern Syria and northern Arabia, bordering the Jordan River. Its indigenous population is described as "East" Jordanians, as compared to the "Palestinian" Jordanians who moved into Jordan after the 1948 Arab-Israeli War.

under heavy attack by Israeli F-35's, Jordan's king Hashem tries desperately to raise Leiberman on the phone, but he finds that all his communications have been jammed, likely by hostile electronic countermeasures, he concludes. In fact, Israeli electronic warfare units are very busy today, ensuring that no potential adversary—whether any Syrian/Iranian forces east of the Golan Heights, the small Egyptian force in Sinai, or the Jordanian military—is able to pass information or orders up or down the chain of command. Units in the field or at their bases have little idea of what is happening and receive no instructions from higher command; military headquarters know next to nothing of the status of their units and have no way to send them orders.

Cyberwarfare experts at Mossad—who in 2010 inflicted the Stuxnet worm on the Iranian nuclear program—have unleashed viruses and other malware against communications and power networks in Jordan, Lebanon, Syria, and Egypt. Civilian mobile phone, landline, and internet networks crash one after the other, and many cities go dark as their power grids fail, all without a single Israeli bomb having touched the first generating plant, switching station, or power line.

Washington, DC, USA
2:30 a.m., Thursday, October 13

In Washington, an exhausted and weary president is still in the Oval Office, huddled with Davis, Allen, Williams, and Secretary of State John Alteman. Allen just moments before had brought in information showing that the Israelis are attacking Palestinian cities in the West Bank and also commencing air raids on Jordan. "What are these guys up to?" exclaims Stayer. "Get me Leiberman again."

Within minutes he is put through on the phone. "Mr. Prime Minister," Stayer virtually shouts into the handset, "what are you doing attacking the West Bank and Jordan? Both the Jordanian government and the Palestinian Authority are America's close friends, and also Israel's. Are you guys going nuts?"

"Mr. President," Leiberman responds, "the whole region is going nuts. Hamas, which initiated an attack against us, is attempting a takeover of the West Bank, and you know that we can never allow that to happen, so we have to preempt them. The Palestinian Authority is powerless against Hamas, and we will not under any circumstances permit the West Bank to become another Islamist terrorist enclave on our border with their operatives lobbing missiles at our capital whenever they want. Also, we have received reliable intelligence from Amman that King Hashem, in a desperate move reminiscent of King Hussein's assault on Israel in 1967, feels that he has no choice but to attack us in order to preserve his throne. Demonstrations in support of the Palestinians are starting to break out in Amman, and the king feels he must either take action against us or else be overthrown.

"At this stage, Mr. President, Israel is fighting a potential three-front war, and that does not include the possibility of the Iranians jumping in directly if they decide to launch their missiles at us. Under such circumstances, we can hardly afford to take any chances. Jordan, at the end of the day, has a well-trained army of one hundred thousand men plus hundreds of tanks—clearly she can cause us damage if she wants to. We cannot and will not allow one Israeli to be killed unnecessarily by any of these Arabs, and hence we are taking preemptive military action against them. I also, frankly, cannot rely on any US assurances, Mr. President. Iran has just walked all over your Arab clients, and you're unable to do anything to help them. In this volatile environment, anything can happen, so we must err on the side of extreme caution and defend ourselves. Until we get this whole situation under control, we will attack any Arab country or organization that we think harbors the slightest intention of attacking us. As we speak, I am in a bunker beneath my office building as missiles are raining down on my population centers. I am not sitting in the safety of the White House, Mr. President, so I will thank you for appreciating that my perspective here must by sheer necessity be slightly different from yours. Now if you will excuse me, I have a war to attend to." At that, the discussion ends. Leiberman puts down the phone and turns around to face his aides, a smug look on his face. "I gave it to the son of a bitch this time," he crows.

Stayer hangs up the receiver on his end and groans. "What is happening over there? Why on earth would the Israelis think Jordan would attack them? What are our people telling us, Richard?"

"Sir," the CIA director responds, "it's all very confusing. We've learned that the Israelis are employing massive electronic countermeasures and apparent cyberattacks against all the surrounding countries in order to disrupt communications, so we can't even get through to talk to the Jordanians. Our embassy in Amman has been trying to call the king for the past hour. We aren't even able to get a read on communications within the Jordanian military. So we're not sure what's happening. The Israelis are probably overreacting. King Hashem is not stupid; he would be insane to take on the Israelis as he knows full well the price Hussein paid for his own folly in 1967."

"Yes," Davis interrupts, "but today he is a frightened man, threatened and very worried by the surging popular dissent in Jordan that is fueled by spreading populism across the region. These Arab demonstrations and protests have panicked all of those Arab rulers, and who knows, maybe some of Hashem's people convinced him to make a token military gesture of Arab solidarity, to which the Israelis are now nervously overreacting. After all, history is full of wars that have been provoked by leaders misreading each other's intentions."

"Well, this guy Leiberman is difficult enough to deal with in normal times," Stayer interjects in exasperation, "so trying to get through his thick skull now is an exercise in futility."

It is at this moment that the president receives a call from Eric Adams, the Republican Speaker of the House of Representatives. "Mr. President," he says, "we are very concerned about what is happening in the Middle East. We believe Israel deserves our unqualified thanks and appreciation for taking down Iran's nuclear facilities. They did the whole free world a great service and should be recognized for that. We also want to make sure that America will stand 100 percent behind the Israelis in this difficult time as all their neighbors attack them."

"Mr. Speaker," the president responds dryly, "we always stand by the Israelis as you very well know, and we don't intend this time to behave any differently. What concerns me is that the Israelis may be making matters worse by misinterpreting and then overreacting to signals from their neighbors, and consequently they're getting themselves, the United States, and the world into an even bigger mess."

"Well, sir," the Speaker responds, "this is no time to second-guess our allies in Israel. They are on the ground and are now under attack, and they deserve our explicit and unquestioning support. They live in a very dangerous neighborhood as you know. Better that they be safe than sorry. The administration should be on notice, Mr. President, that Congress expects unqualified support to be extended to our Israeli friends and also that Congress will vehemently resist any wavering of such support. To repeat, this is hardly the time, in their moment of peril, to second-guess our friends and allies."

Stayer hangs up the phone, already exhausted by a very long day that shows no signs of ending soon.

Davis then puts in front of him an op-ed due to come out in the morning's *Washington Post*, titled "Time to Rethink US Policy in the Persian Gulf" and written by a prominent former secretary of state.

> The Iranians' and Iraqis' military action to protect the Shia minority in Kuwait must be evaluated in a balanced and calm manner. The atrocious terrorist attack on Shia worshippers in Kuwait City was just the latest event in an historic pattern of discrimination and repression that the Arab Shia have endured under Sunni rule. The United States has to appreciate and respect that our Iraqi allies, particularly, are extremely upset by this tragedy. The US, after all, now has a "constituency" of twenty million Iraqi Shia, and we cannot lightly dismiss their passionate concern for their fellow Shia in the Gulf. Iran's intervention, particularly in this vital oil-producing area, is very dangerous, and as a result, America has obviously found herself in a very difficult position. We need to take a step back and evaluate the situation very carefully, instead of reacting impulsively and taking immediate military action, which would further inflame the region and may very well cause further damage to America's interests. We should ask ourselves this question: Has the time come for America to reassess our entire structure of alliances in this region and establish a new structure, one that accounts for the heretofore disregarded fact that the Shia make up the majority population around the whole Persian Gulf?

When Stayer finishes reading the op-ed, Davis adds, "And that is not all, sir. A Washington-based think tank called the Gulf Policy Institute, run by Shia dissidents from Saudi Arabia, has already sent emails to all members of Congress and key journalists, enclosing a detailed file of what they allege is massive discrimination and repression by the ruling Sunni elite against the two million Shia in the Gulf countries. The think tank has called a press conference, to be held at Capitol Hill in the morning under the sponsorship of two congressmen, one a Republican and the other a Democrat, to elaborate on this point and call for noninterference in the Iraqi-Iranian liberation of 'their people.'" After a pause he adds, "Well, it looks like the circus is about to begin. We'd better get prepared for Congress, the media, interest groups, talking heads, and all the armchair generals to pile into us over the next few days."

Washington, DC, USA
6 a.m., Thursday, October 13

After having taken a short nap, the president and his advisors, many of whom had spent the night in the White House, reconvene for breakfast. At this point, the secretary of the Treasury joins the group. "Mr. President," he begins, "at this moment, our number one priority needs to be the economy, both our domestic and the global economy. We are now actually staring global economic Armageddon in the face. The introduction of nuclear weapons into the Persian Gulf followed by another Arab-Israeli war on top of the ongoing Iranian invasion of Arabia is, quite evidently, beyond the financial markets' capacity to absorb. Markets are now assuming a total cutoff of Middle Eastern oil from the Persian Gulf to their main markets in Asia. The Chinese, Indians, Japanese, Koreans, and Taiwanese have been talking to us all night, and they are in a total panic. They had to suspend trading today in their financial markets to keep things from melting down completely. Based on what happened with our markets yesterday, I am not surprised. They're imploring us to do something to instill confidence before their economies collapse. It is my strong recommendation that we take action; we must do *something!*"

"What do you recommend?" Stayer asks him.

"Well, sir, first of all we need to open our strategic oil reserves and flood the petroleum market. We have a six-month supply in reserve, and releasing it should help calm investor sentiment. Then we have to basically guarantee the integrity of the US financial system by stating that our government will stand completely behind the solvency of its financial institutions and also support global liquidity. This has to be followed by similar actions from the Europeans, the Japanese, and the Chinese. We are coordinating with them all at the moment. Now, what I suggest, Mr. President, is that you address the nation from the Oval Office ASAP, set out these steps, and try to convey the confidence the United States has in the integrity of our financial system, as well as in our own and the world's capacity to weather this crisis. Then hope for the best in Asia and on Wall Street today. No more can be done now beyond taking these steps—nothing except pray, sir, if I may be plain."

"And what about the Middle East?" Davis interjects to ask the president. "What do we do there?"

"I say we wait and see," Stayer responds. "Not much we are able to do now. We can hardly commit troops to make a difference on the ground, and we have our hands full trying to keep the bottom from falling out of our economy, so let's deal with that issue now and then wait and see how things play out on the ground over there."

"Well, sir, we have had virtually every Gulf leader on the line over the past few hours, asking to speak with you. What should we tell them?"

"Pass them on to the vice president or to John," Stayer responds, giving a nod in the direction of his secretary of state, who answers by nodding back. "They can tell them that we are studying the situation carefully and will get back in touch with them soon. Now let me get my speechwriters in here and focus on constructing a solid message to deliver to the public. Hopefully we can save our economy from imploding."

Negev Desert, southern Israel
1 p.m., Thursday, October 13

The Israelis have been pummeling Gaza for over ten hours, and the narrow strip of land is now little more than a smoking ruin devoid of life, save for the IDF soldiers slowly and deliberately sweeping south to conduct a final clearance and then secure the southern border against any Palestinians who may attempt reentry. An hour past noon, three Israeli mechanized battalions staged on Israel's southern border receive terse instructions by radio. Plumes of exhaust rise into the clear air as the ranks of armored vehicles throttle up and race into the open desert of Sinai. Their objective is the removal of the Egyptian forces located there.

Jerusalem, Israel
1:30 p.m., Thursday, October 13

Meanwhile, at the Ministry of Foreign Affairs in Jerusalem, Foreign Minister Shoval summons the Egyptian ambassador to Israel, Khalid Bassiouni, to his office (the Israeli ambassador to Egypt had been wisely pulled out of Cairo the day before). Bassiouni, a veteran diplomat based in Tel Aviv for over eight years, is a darling of Israeli society. While Israel's ambassador in Cairo is shunned by Egyptian society and hence mixes virtually exclusively with other diplomats, Israeli society can hardly get enough of Bassiouni, who is the honored guest of every socialite and hostess from Eilat to the Golan Heights. Consequently, Bassiouni is used to being received by all Israelis with great warmth and respect, so he is shocked at the cold, arrogant tone of his host today.

"Mr. Ambassador," a cocky Shoval begins, "you will note that we have unleashed our nuclear missiles upon Iran. That has resulted in retaliatory attacks on our citizenry by Hezbollah and your ally Hamas. I don't want to get into a discussion about the whole region now but instead wish to focus purely on Egypt and her behavior. Your government, dominated again now by the Muslim Brotherhood, has effectively torn up the peace treaty between our two countries. You have been unconditionally supporting Hamas, you have stopped supplying us with gas—which is in direct contravention of the treaty—and you have allowed not only arms to flow to Hamas but also terrorists to operate against us from Sinai with virtual impunity. When Menachem Begin returned Sinai to Anwar Sadat in 1979, we expected to achieve total peace with Egypt in return. Now, decades later, particularly after the Egyptian people reelected the Muslim Brotherhood, Egypt has completely failed to hold up her end of the bargain. Given all of these factors, our government has decided that we have little choice but to retaliate by abrogating this now meaningless treaty. The cabinet, today, has consequently approved not only the total destruction of Hamas and the terrorist infrastructure they have built up in Gaza but also the complete reoccupation of Sinai. To be plain, we have reached the conclusion that we cannot guarantee the security of our people in the south of Israel without the benefit of the strategic depth which the Sinai Peninsula affords. So, your government has a simple choice, Mr. Ambassador: It can accept this fact and reconcile itself to the permanent loss of Sinai to Israel, or it can declare war. Such a war, I assure you, will be nuclear. We are determined to, once and for all, secure our children's future in their ancestral land. Hence, going forward we have decided that we will destroy anybody who dares to stand in our way. You should have no doubt in your mind that *we will not hesitate to wipe Cairo off the face of the earth if we have to.* I think the events of the last few hours should convince your government and your people of our seriousness in this regard. Also, you should have no illusions that US or international intervention can stop us. We are fighting for our ultimate survival and will do what we have to do irrespective of any pressure from our allies."

Bassiouni, nearly speechless in the face of Shoval's audacity, tries to get a word in edgewise. "Your analysis is completely wrong, Mr. Shoval, and I must point out ..."

The foreign minister talks over him. "Now, I have not called you here to debate this message, but simply to dictate it to you clearly so you can convey it to your government immediately. We will trade peace with Egypt for your survival as a nation. *No more of the 'land for peace'* nonsense. That formula is dead as far as the government of Israel is concerned. From now on, what we offer is *'peace for peace.'* If you want to survive as a nation, you will have to accept Israel in her present form and with Sinai as an integral and permanent part of Israel. The choice belongs to your government and to the people of Egypt.

"You should also know that after our meeting, this message will be leaked to the media so that your public also receives it loud and clear. Let your people fully comprehend what is at stake, and then we will see how eager they are to continue their demonstrations against us. I also suggest that your government begin making preparations to receive the Egyptian population currently living east of the Suez Canal—*urgent* preparations.

Now, either you can help evacuate your people, or else the IDF will remove them in the same way that we are clearing Gaza, the West Bank, and south Lebanon. The choice is yours, but rest assured: one way or the other, all Egyptians will be removed from the Sinai Peninsula. The era of playing games in the Middle East is over, Mr. Ambassador. I suggest you run home now and call your government." The stunned ambassador, aghast at the message he has just received, stands, turns, and disgustedly leaves the foreign minister's office.

Sinai, Egypt
2 p.m., Thursday, October 13

In Sinai, the IDF forces deployed against the three Egyptian military bases that hold the small contingents of troops allowed in Sinai under the terms of the 1979 peace treaty coordinate simultaneous approaches to their targets. Each camp finds itself surrounded by an Israeli mechanized battalion, trapped in a ring of steel formed by the Merkava main battle tanks of the 75th, 82nd, and 198th Battalions. The Egyptian soldiers at one installation decide to resist, only to die in flames as support from the Israeli Air Force rains high explosive and napalm munitions on the close confines of the camp and as the 105-millimeter main guns of the Merkavas, with unerring precision, decimate what remains. At the other two camps, the Egyptians offer only token resistance, overcome with shock at the unexpected Israeli assault and beset by increasing fear as rumors circulate not only of the nuclear strikes on Iran but also of the merciless pounding inflicted on Southern Lebanon.

Once the task force commanders pass word that the Egyptian camps have been secured, infantrymen of the elite Golani Brigade are helicoptered in to take control of all choke points across the Suez Canal. Military police move in to take custody of the disarmed Egyptian forces, numbering fewer than a thousand, who are to be trucked to the border and unceremoniously repatriated.

Meanwhile, the Eighty-Second Battalion, which cleared the northernmost camp, races west to bolster the defenses along the canal and help dissuade any Egyptian shot callers who may be reconsidering the decision to surrender the Sinai Peninsula. Two other battalions have been tasked with ensuring that the Egyptians clear their population from Sinai with alacrity, their presence there providing a visible reminder of Israeli military force and the implied threat that they will repeat the clearing actions conducted in Gaza, the West Bank, and south Lebanon if the Egyptians don't carry out the task themselves. One battalion moves north to Romani, Bir Qatia, Qantara Sharqiya, and the environs of Port Said on the east bank of Suez; the other heads to Ash Shatt, Uyun Musa, and Ras Misalla across the canal from the city of Suez at the head of the Gulf of Suez. A fourth unit, an infantry battalion, having been dispatched from its staging area outside Eilat shortly after the mechanized battalions crossed the border, now arrives in the resort area of Sharm el-Sheikh.

Much of the Egyptian population is close to the canal, which makes their removal a relatively quick process, though the Egyptian police have to employ tear gas and batons more than once to evict those who would rather stay and fight the Israelis. Egyptian military forces deploy to the border, but their job is to ensure that dislocated Egyptians remain west of the canal, not to challenge the Israelis. The units have their hands full in dealing with massive protests as thousands take to the streets demanding war with Israel. Buses, trucks, taxis, and private autos begin shuttling the residents of the towns along the shore of the Gulf of Suez north.

In the end, the process will take nearly three days—though as more and more television footage of the devastation in Lebanon,

Gaza, and the West Bank hits the airwaves, most of the remaining Egyptians will grow less resistant to departing—and finally the Israeli occupation of Sinai will be completed for the third time in history.

Chapter 6: Pakistan to the Rescue

Nine generals and the intelligence chief are now gathered with Afzal in the conference room next to his office at the military cantonment in Rāwalpindi, which houses army headquarters. "Gentlemen," Afzal begins, "I will get to the point immediately. You all know what has been happening in the Persian Gulf over the past two days. King Mashari spoke to me yesterday from Mecca, where he and his government have taken refuge. He has formally requested that Pakistan use her nuclear missile capabilities to stop the Iranians. I promised him I would do my best and reply to his request as soon as possible." Afzal, a cautious and highly decorated officer in his early sixties, tries to present this volatile information matter-of-factly to the group.

"We must realize that the Iranians are poised to swallow the whole of Arabia and wrest control of all of Arabia's oil. The Israelis, in a cynical move, only targeted the nuclear facilities, effectively allowing the Iranians the freedom to continue their invasion. The Americans, in turn, are frozen into inaction, so nobody is stopping the Iranians. If they succeed, not only will they become the undisputed power in the Gulf, but also they will effectively assume leadership of Islam and control the world's oil. The Arabs have probably faced nothing this perilous since the Mongols' invasion in the Middle Ages. The political map of our whole area is about to change. Now, unfortunately, the *only* way Iran can be stopped is with nuclear weapons." Afzal is pacing while the other ten men sit at a U-shaped table, carefully hanging onto his every word.

"We have been studying options over the last few hours, and to be plain, there is little that can be done at this point to force the Iranians to withdraw from Arabia short of hitting Tehran and thereby crippling the heart of their state, bringing this Persian juggernaut to a halt. The Iranians are already all over the oil fields, and they have taken over Kuwait, the Saudi Eastern Province, and Bahrain. If they are not stopped now, they will easily move on to Riyadh and Mecca, as well as Qatar, the United Arab Emirates, and Oman. The Americans, taken by surprise just like the rest of us, have been unable to do anything so far, and our intelligence officers tell me that they see little the Americans *can* do against these hordes of Iranians and Iraqis storming Arabia, even if they did want to intervene in some way.

"The problem here is that the Iranians are rapidly creating facts on the ground, and the Americans may eventually decide to accept these and deal with a de facto Iranian empire rather than undertake another massive war in the Gulf, the consequences of which would be uncertain and very costly. Frankly, even if the Americans wanted to attack, we are not sure how such a thing could be done without destroying the whole infrastructure of Arabian oil and hence removing a quarter of global oil production from the market for years. It is readily apparent that the Iranians have made a huge gamble, and as of now it looks like they have pulled it off." None of the men interrupt Afzal with questions or comments as they process what they have just been told and think through the ramifications for Pakistan.

"All of this leads me to conclude that the only option left to stop the Iranians cold is for us to unleash a nuclear attack on Tehran. This is a terrible step, one of historic significance, and as such it will require our unanimous agreement. I cannot take individual responsibility—neither in front of my people nor in the face of history—for such a momentous decision."

The generals are quiet for a while as they ponder the enormous significance of what they have just heard. They are all smart enough to realize the substantial rewards that will accrue to Pakistan, and even to them personally, for saving Arabia from the Iranians, although it shocks them that the sole means to accomplishing this end must be a nuclear attack on Iran.

Then, General Zia Afridi, the Karachi-based V Corps commander who has to deal with continuous ethnic and religious-sectarian strife in Pakistan's megacity of twelve million people, asks, "Are we not risking jumping into a sectarian Sunni-Shiite war here, which Pakistan can hardly afford to do? Remember that 20 percent of our population is Shia, and we cannot be perceived as taking any particular side in a sectarian conflict."

"That is a good point," Afzal responds, "and we have to weigh that issue very carefully. I think, however, that we can successfully frame this issue very much in an Arabian/Iranian context and remind our people of Pakistan's vital interests in the Gulf. Millions of Pakistanis, both Sunni and Shia, have relatives working in or dealing with the Gulf, and surely they'll realize that an Iranian takeover will jeopardize everything for them. We have billions of dollars in annual workers' remittances that come in from the Gulf, and this is before we count all the financial aid and other support we get from the Saudis and the Gulf states." Afridi serves himself a cup of tea while carefully listening to Afzal.

"If the Iranians colonize the Gulf, they will also move in and settle millions of their own people, who will inevitably take the millions of jobs Pakistanis now hold in that region. Also, our population will be horrified by the possibility of a takeover of Mecca and Medina by the Iranian mullahs, so we should receive express and enthusiastic public support, particularly from the powerful Islamist political parties. Look, gentlemen, the people of Pakistan will realize that we have a huge stake in the status quo of Arabia. The Gulf's becoming an Iranian colony would be an unqualified disaster for Pakistan."

Now that Afridi had broken the spellbound silence and opened a dialogue, the others begin to relax a bit and also serve themselves tea. Then they start to hash out the pros and cons of Afzal's proposal. After considerable discussion, they all agree with Afzal that an empowered "Persian empire" in control of Arabia and gorging on Arab oil would spell disaster for Pakistan, and this fact alone justifies drastic action on their part.

"Funnily enough," Afzal says, picking up the conversational thread, "the Israelis have done us a favor, because in introducing nuclear weapons into the region, they have broken the nuclear taboo. If we use our weapons now, we will not be fingered by the world as the first in this conflict to do so. Also, the elimination of Iran's capability is a very good thing for all of us." This new perspective is well received by the generals.

General Afridi speaks up again with a word of caution: "Gentlemen, while I think we all agree that a nuclear strike will probably be necessary in the end, surely we are not contemplating simply launching an attack on Tehran without warning. Even the Americans toward the end of World War Two presented an ultimatum to the Japanese almost two weeks before destroying Hiroshima. I don't think we can do any less in this situation, and certainly not after the Israelis have now launched their own attack on Iran, unless we wish the entire Muslim world to compare us to them."

Afzal strokes his chin and nods slowly. "You make a valid point. We should not take such drastic action without giving the Iranians an opportunity to back down. I have little hope they will do so, of course, but at least we will have made the offer."

Lieutenant General Muhammad Pasha, Pakistan's key liaison with Washington, also the powerful head of the Inter-Services Intelligence Directorate, which is the military's intelligence arm, reminds all present that Pakistan can hardly embark on a nuclear attack without at least first alerting, and preferably consulting with, Washington. "Tendering an ultimatum to Iran will also give us time to manage this situation with the US. We have to make sure the Americans realize, once their satellites pick up indications that our silos are being readied for launch, that the missile will be headed for Tehran, not India. The US needs to inform and reassure the Indians. We don't want those in India jumping to the wrong conclusions, thinking that we are targeting them and therefore reacting by launching their nuclear missiles at us."

"An excellent point," they all agree.

General Afridi adds that the Indians, whose political and economic interests in the Gulf are also substantial, will likewise be very concerned by Iran's actions. "In addition, we cannot afford to be on the wrong side of America's will on something as momentous as a nuclear attack. Our relationship with Washington is delicate enough, and we can't afford a break with them if they oppose such a move."

"The problem," Afzal adds, "is that this strike is now *the only option*. Everyone in this room knows this to be true. I think—I hope—that the Americans will be all too willing to let us do their dirty work in this matter; certainly that's been the case in Afghanistan through two wars. But what if they have no stomach for the second use of nuclear weapons in a matter of days? We cannot allow their reticence to leave Iran free to dominate Arabia."

"Then we present them with a fait accompli," Pasha interjects, slamming his fist onto the tabletop. "We issue the ultimatum— and only then do we consult with the Americans, informing them that we will launch against Tehran if Iran does not comply, and asking that they make appropriate notifications to the Indian government. We simply force their hand."

A murmur of assent ripples through the group. The generals then begin drafting an ultimatum, calling for the immediate withdrawal of Iran from all occupied territories in Arabia, to be issued at 8 p.m. Tehran time—exactly forty-eight hours after Motahidi's speech announcing Iran's attack. Once the countdown to the deadline begins, Pasha will discreetly consult with the Americans.

Islamabad, Pakistan
9:30 p.m., Thursday, October 13

Having called a press conference, the Pakistani president now steps to the podium, blinking a couple of times from the glare of numerous television cameras pointed his way. The crowd of journalists—attracted to the press conference by carefully timed leaks over the past few hours that the forthcoming announcement would be one of major significance—is uncharacteristically hushed. Behind the president stand Afzal and the officers of the general staff in a single rank, shoulder to shoulder, a silent but implicit confirmation that the impending announcement has their blessing.

"For the past forty-eight hours," the president intones gravely, reading from a prepared statement, "the people of Pakistan have watched with sadness and growing concern the violence sweeping the shores of the Persian Gulf. Despite the terrible loss of life suffered as a result of the cowardly attack on the Al Abbas Mosque in Kuwait City, we believe that Iran has far overstepped her bounds. Her subsequent invasion of Kuwait, Saudi Arabia, and Bahrain—to say nothing of the threat she now poses to the other Gulf states—goes well beyond reacting to any provocation, real or manufactured. Iran has violated the norms of acceptable behavior and international law with this gross, unprovoked aggression against her fellow Muslims and neighbors, including the Kingdom of Saudi Arabia, the birthplace of Islam and host of its holiest cities. Pakistan cannot and will not accept this. It is our duty to defend our Muslim brothers in Arabia and protect our holiest sites. We can never allow them to be invaded by anybody, whatever the pretext.

"We therefore call upon the Islamic Republic of Iran to immediately and without precondition begin the withdrawal of her forces from Arabia and to cease any and all support to groups engaged in domestic insurrection against the legitimate governments of the region.

"We expect Iran to promptly respond to our ultimatum and announce her immediate withdrawal from all occupied GCC[23] territories. Should Iran fail to do so by no later than twelve noon Greenwich Mean Time on Friday the fourteenth of October, Pakistan will take any and all action deemed necessary—including the most drastic steps—in order to end this act of naked aggression."

---

[23] GCC designates the Gulf Cooperation Council. Member countries of this council are Saudi Arabia, Kuwait, Bahrain, Qatar, the UAE, and Oman.

Ignoring the tidal wave of shouted questions that break out in the seconds after he concludes his statement, the president steps away from the podium and quickly vanishes through a side door. Afzal glances at his colleagues and nods once, his expression grave, and the generals likewise file out of the room.

Washington, DC, USA
12:30 p.m., Thursday, October 13

At the White House, Stayer has concluded his speech to the American people only a few minutes before, and the camera crew is just now wheeling its equipment out of the Oval Office when CIA director Allen rushes in. After he greets both the secretary of state and the secretary of defense, who are there with Stayer, he delivers the news. "Mr. President, the Pakistanis have just informed us that King Mashari of Saudi Arabia spoke to General Afzal and asked the Pakistanis to nuke the Iranians. The ultimatum that they issued to the Iranians earlier today was nothing more than political cover—they're going to do it if Iran doesn't budge, which, judging by how quickly the Iranian Foreign Ministry repudiated Pakistan's demands, is pretty damned likely. Afzal says they have no choice given their huge interests in the Gulf and their fear of an emergent Iranian imperial monster taking over the whole of Arabia. They understandably wanted us to know well in advance, and they also want us to alert and reassure the Indians. What do you think?"

Stayer, taken aback by the question and its enormous implications, inhales deeply and looks at the others in amazement. "Well, this is certainly an unexpected development," he exclaims while breathing out.

After a few minutes of silence, Williams is the first to respond. "You know what," he offers to everyone in the room, "that actually may not be such a crazy idea. It is certainly the only thing that can now stop the Iranians in their tracks. We have no way ourselves of stopping them, and the United States can hardly be the country that nukes Iran. But one of their fellow Muslim countries doing it—that is a totally different story. Such a step, however horrible, may actually be the only possible solution on the table."

Allen nods his head slowly, indicating both his agreement with Williams's conclusions and his near-disbelief. However unimaginable this situation would have been just a few days prior, here the president's administration finds itself debating the costs-to-benefits of a nuclear attack.

John Alteman clears his throat. "Gentlemen, am I understanding this correctly? We're about to willingly condone the use of nuclear weapons? Not only would that go against our nonproliferation policy, but it would also paint the US as totally hypocritical when it comes to protecting our own interests."

Williams replies to Alteman, "John, I appreciate your concerns, as I think all of us here do. But if you think about this, we are actually now being presented with a potential solution to our dilemma where, frankly, no other immediate solution exists. The Iranian threat can now be eliminated, and at the same time the US won't have to do much more than give the nod in order for this to be accomplished. We give the okay to Pakistan under the table, as it were, and we can retain plausible deniability! The Pakistanis will be doing us all a great favor. Otherwise, we are stuck with an Iranian empire in charge of the world's oil, period!"

"I need to make it very clear," Allen quickly interjects, "that the Pakistanis didn't call asking for our permission. They were polite, but the language that was used made it overwhelmingly obvious that this is *going to happen*. We might be able to stop them, but there are no guarantees."

Stayer nods as he absorbs Allen's analysis. "In any event, I agree with Hank," the president says after a few moments. Then turning to face Alteman square-on, he adds, "We really have no other option, John; either it's this, or else these mullahs have the world by the balls."

"I guess we have no other choice," Alteman replies, sighing. "What a horrible proposition to have to accept."

"Well, I guess that's what a president is paid for," Stayer gravely responds, "ultimately having to make the impossible calls." He then turns to Allen, grimly giving his assent. "Richard, inform the Pakistanis that while our official policy remains firmly against deployment and the use of nuclear weapons by anybody, unofficially—and obviously off the record—the United States takes no position on how they deal with Iran."

Allen then leaves the Oval Office and makes his way to the NSC offices in the West Wing, where he uses a secure line to call the embassy in Islamabad. He speaks to the CIA station chief there, who is Pasha's contact. Allen instructs the station chief to meet immediately with General Pasha and convey the president's message. He then hangs up with Islamabad and places a similar call to the US Embassy in New Delhi, instructing the CIA station chief at that location to alert the Indians to what is happening.

Rāwalpindi, Pakistan
11:45 p.m., Thursday, October 13

In Rāwalpindi, the generals anxiously await the Americans' response and are relieved to finally hear word from Pasha. Needing no more encouragement, they authorize the attack. The decision is made to launch only one nuclear missile at Tehran, and the orders are issued to prepare that missile for launch, a process that will take a number of hours to complete. The Pakistani objective here is not to destroy the whole city but, rather, to shock the leadership and also the military to such a degree as to make them realize that failure to withdraw immediately from Arabia will lead to further nuclear attacks.

Once the order is disseminated to all concerned personnel, the process of transporting and assembling the necessary components gets under way. The decades-long instability of Pakistan's political environment, combined with American concerns about the security of the Pakistani nuclear arsenal in the wake of 9/11, had resulted in the country's storing the nuclear arsenal in such a manner that exceeds security concerns and indeed approaches paranoia. Put simply, Pakistan's weapons are stored in a state of disassembly and across multiple locations. The fissile material—highly enriched uranium in most cases, although Pakistan does have a few plutonium-based weapons—is stored separately from the explosives packages used to trigger a nuclear reaction, and both of these are warehoused separately from the warheads and launch vehicles. Collecting the various components from their secure storage locations and assembling a complete weapon—in this case, a Hatf-6 intermediate-range ballistic missile capable of covering the nearly thirteen hundred miles to Tehran—is a time-consuming process that requires multiple cross-checks, all conducted under airtight security. In addition to this, a second missile is also prepped as a contingency against a malfunction of the primary weapon.

The Pakistani weapon is small with a yield roughly equivalent to that of the American weapon used against Hiroshima—though "small" is a relative term as that attack obliterated everything within a one-mile radius of ground zero and immediately killed some eighty thousand people with tens of thousands dying later from radiation poisoning. Still, notwithstanding the destruction this will cause, the result Pakistan seeks is an Iranian withdrawal of troops, not total demolition of its capital city. It is the generals' hope that one Pakistani nuke will be sufficient to put an end to the Iranian invasion of Arabia.

Tehran, Iran
3:37 p.m., Friday, October 14

The supreme leader is at work in his quarters and in an optimistic mood, surrounded by his key aides and assistants. He dismisses the Pakistani ultimatum as a "hollow threat." "These generals are in the pay of the Arabs," he tells Jalili. "They have to make noise, but they will never dare attack us. We share a huge border with them, as well as retain close ties to their Shia. Also, a war with us would finally finish off Pakistan as an independent state because India will take it as a heaven-sent opportunity to jump in and dismember the Pakistani state once and for all. So don't worry about them; let them bark as much as they want."

He then reviews reports coming in from the field confirming that his troops are already well embedded in strategic locations across the Saudi oil-producing areas and are in total control of all major cities and towns on the Persian Gulf coast from Kuwait to Bahrain. Also, the word from his advisors, particularly Moslehi, who has been working the phones in Washington, is that the Americans, as expected, are overwhelmed and unsure of what to do. The chance of an American military intervention is diminishing very fast. "We are about to witness the birth of the new Iranian Empire that will become a world superpower," he tells his aides with satisfaction. "The Almighty has not let us down, and nobody will be able to stop us now."

At thirty-seven minutes after three in the afternoon, on the occasion of the second use of nuclear weapons in anger since the end of World War II and less than forty-eight hours after Israel unleashed its own attack, the Pakistani nuclear missile detonates a few hundred meters above eastern Tehran, where the cluster of buildings housing the supreme leader and other key elements of Iran's leadership are located. The emerging Iranian imperial dream is instantly decapitated in a mushroom cloud of atomic debris and radioactive smoke.

Chapter 7: The Day After

Saturday, October 15

On the day after, the world wakes up to an Israel ethnically cleansed of its Arabs and firmly in control of a territory four times its original size; a Jordan taken over by the Palestinians; and an Islamic Republic of Iran brought to its knees by Israeli and Pakistani nuclear missiles.

In Tehran, a coup d'état takes place. A group of officers from the Revolutionary Guard move in and assume power amid the smoldering wreckage of Iran's capital city. Their leader declares martial law across the whole country, and the military junta accuses the mullahs of insane adventurism, holding them responsible for the catastrophe that has befallen their nation. Key mullahs and figures from the former regime who survived the attack on Tehran are hunted down and eliminated.

The junta then orders an immediate withdrawal of all Iranian forces from Arabia. It also issues an urgent appeal to the UN for help in coping with its massive humanitarian and ecological disaster. The UN eagerly complies and launches, with the assistance of NATO, a massive airlift to rush medical and decontamination personnel and equipment to Tehran and other stricken areas.

In Iraq, Prime Minister al-Mosawi, with an embarrassing political, diplomatic, and military debacle on his hands, and under accusation by members of his parliament of gross misjudgment, appears on state television and, with a straight face, strongly condemns the deposed government of the Islamic Republic of Iran for having "illegally" invaded Iraqi territory and attacked Iraq's "brothers," Kuwait, Saudi Arabia, and Bahrain. He then pledges to arrest and bring to justice any Iraqi "traitors" who participated in this outrage.

In Jerusalem, Prime Minister Leiberman receives in his office Marwan Hamoudi, the young and charismatic Palestinian leader whom he has just had released from an Israeli prison. Hamoudi, who has been called by many the "Palestinian Mandela," is now about to be sent on his way to assume leadership of the newly formed Republic of Palestine, previously the Hashemite Kingdom of Jordan. Leiberman assures him of full Israeli and US support.

The situation in Amman, Jordan, is chaotic; government no longer functions, and mobs now control the streets. The Israelis, however, having anticipated such a situation, now deploy a requisite security force to ensure that the new Hamoudi government is able to take control. An elite Israeli unit of border police and Shin Bet intelligence operatives, who have years of experience controlling the occupied territories in Palestine, lead a force of twenty thousand troops, previously members of the Palestinian Authority's Preventive Security Force, to secure Amman. This force, which the Israelis and Americans have been building up and training for decades, will now be put to good use in establishing the foundation of state security for the new Palestinian government.

Hamoudi arrives by helicopter at Amman's InterContinental Hotel, which Israeli paratroopers have completely secured and converted into a makeshift temporary government headquarters. Camera crews are already on the scene, having been alerted prior to his arrival, and Hamoudi appears live on television from the hotel's lobby to declare the establishment of the Republic of Palestine. He also declares that his government will adopt a "right of return" that will extend full Palestinian citizenship to all members of the Palestinian diaspora. In addition, he calls for national reconciliation with the East Jordanian population and announces that strict punishment will be imposed for any acts of violence committed by the majority population against the minority East Jordanians. His team and the Israelis are conscious of the mistakes that Jerry Bremer, America's first proconsul of Iraq, made when he dissolved the Iraqi Army and bureaucracy, pushing many of them into armed opposition, so he also assures all members of the security forces and all employees of the former Jordanian government that they will retain their jobs.

Following this statement and the subsequent imposition of security in Amman over the next few days, as looters and vigilantes are shot on sight, things start to fall into place at a reasonably quick pace. Government employees begin reporting to work, and calm returns to the streets.

Within days, the United States, the European Union, Russia, China, and Japan will all recognize the new Republic of Palestine and announce a willingness to extend an emergency aid package to help the Palestinian economy to its feet. This package will prioritize assistance to help settle the millions of Palestinians who are flocking into their new country.

In Kuwait, eastern Saudi Arabia, and Bahrain, chaos dies down as remnants of the Iranian force and Iraqi militias are wiped out by Saudi forces that have been deployed from Riyadh under an order to reassert control over the Eastern Province. Saudi forces also move in to establish control in Bahrain and Kuwait, where the former governments' authority had totally collapsed after the invasion.

In New York, the UN Security Council members and International Monetary Fund officials have been in constant deliberations since the initial onset of the crisis as the United States, the European Union, China, and Japan take all possible measures to try to calm global financial markets and ensure that these markets, and the entire international financial system along with them, do not collapse. One of these measures was a decision made by President Stayer late Friday, after the Pakistani nuclear strike on Tehran, to suspend trading on all US financial markets until further notice—a step coordinated with and mirrored by governments around the world—to provide a "cooling off" period and prevent an all-out global collapse of these markets.

Afterword

While a "perfect storm" of outlandish events occurring simultaneously, the likes of which I describe in *Arabian War Games*, is of course unlikely, a variation or subset of any of these scenarios is far from impossible.

I wanted, through this work of fiction, to highlight the following points about growing Arabian-Iranian hostilities and the Palestinian-Israeli conflict. I believe that to a large extent, the region's future will depend on how these two issues eventually play out.

Palestine and Israel

The much discussed "peace process" is a red herring since it completely ignores Israel's obsessive determination to maintain its Jewish majority in perpetuity with all its ominous implications. While the world expects Israel to behave in accordance with international law, its actions will instead be driven by the acute sense of paranoia that Zionists, who look at history through the prism of the Jewish people's experience in Christendom, have developed.

At the same time, millions of Palestinians continue to pay the heavy price of living for decades without membership in a nation-state that grants them full citizenship. A people in this day and age needs to have *unqualified* membership in a nation-state in order to prosper. Today, the issue for a person is not so much *land* to live on as it is the appropriate *documentation* needed to operate in a world defined by nationality. Documentation that allows its holders not only to reside in a country but also to study, work, and travel in, and enjoy the dignity that is part and parcel of belonging to, the country in which they live is a categorical imperative.

These Palestinians cannot be allowed to continue to rot in camps as refugees in perpetuity. Arabs, by continuing to keep so many Palestinians as refugees and refusing to grant them the *full rights* of citizenship—so that they may continue to exist as proof of Israel's original sin in expelling them, and also to "protect" the privileged status of existing communities in countries like Jordan and Lebanon—are not only committing a grave injustice but may also be providing the fuel for an upcoming cataclysmic war.

Pretending to wait for diplomacy to solve this problem is to purposefully avoid addressing it, while placing the Palestinians, Jordanians, and Lebanese at serious risk of being on the receiving end of a genocidal war.

Jordan here is the key. Because its population already has a Palestinian majority, Jordan can, in all likelihood, preempt such an Israeli attack by accepting *all* stateless Palestinian refugees as Jordanian citizens. This would have to be done in conjunction with absorbing Gaza and the West Bank into an expanded Jordan–Palestine. This entity would then also extend its citizenship to all Israeli Arabs. *Swapping* the nationality of Israel's Arab-citizen minority with a Jordanian Palestinian one would give the Israelis *a political rather than a military path* to maintaining the Jewish voting majority that they are so dangerously fixated on preserving.

The East Jordanian elites who are so *vehemently opposed* to such an idea need to realize that as they obsess over trying to avoid being "overwhelmed by a sea of Palestinians," their neighbors the Israelis are obsessing over the exact same issue. Here the question will ultimately boil down to this: Who, Israel or Jordan, has more power to push "its Palestinians" onto the other? The Jordanians should have no illusions about the ultimate winner of that contest or, for that matter, the *awful price* that they and their fellow Arabs will inevitably have to pay if the outcome is decided through war!

The Arabian Gulf and Iran

In the Gulf region, Gulf Arabs need to realize that ultimately they can only reliably depend on themselves for survival. To do so, they will need to transform themselves into a larger and more viable political entity that is able to sustain and defend itself. Countries where local citizens are a small minority and whose claim to fame is wealth alone cannot survive long. Survival in a hostile environment requires people, millions of people, to populate your country, operate it, and defend it.

Today's status quo in the Gulf is a "Disneyland" where a little Qatar, for example, because of its wealth, plays at being a world power as its leaders stride confidently across the international stage, even though Qatar is a "state" with *fewer than three hundred thousand citizens!* While the United States may have a base in Qatar, this does not necessarily mean that the US will be willing to lose even a thousand servicemen to defend the Qatari state—or any other Gulf state for that matter—against a predator. Blind faith in the United States' willingness to ensure that three hundred thousand superrich Qataris may continue to enjoy trillions of dollars in oil wealth unmolested is delusional.

Long-term survival can only be ensured if the Gulf states, the GCC members, somehow find a way to merge into a more cohesive entity, maybe even a federal body similar in structure to the current UAE federation. This federation should then also admit Yemen, however distasteful the idea is to the Gulf Arabs of absorbing twenty-five million poor people into the exclusive rich man's club that is the GCC. Yemen cannot continue to be ignored and treated as if it were located on another continent. Positioned at the bottom of the Arabian Peninsula and surrounded on two sides by the sea, Yemen's only land outlet is into the GCC. As Yemen slowly crumbles and maybe even starves when it runs out of water (among its many other problems), its twenty-five-million-plus people will have nowhere to run except north into the GCC. After all, even the United States with all its resources can hardly deter the Mexicans from slowly overwhelming its border states, and Mexico is far from being a Yemen. The GCC has to realize that the Yemenis are coming, whether they like it or not. Yemen is either invited, in an organized manner, to join the "club," or else its people will climb over the walls and, in the process, possibly destroy the cozy and rich "gated community" that is now the GCC.

A GCC federation with Yemen as a member will create a power close to sixty million people strong, benefiting from the strategic geographic depth of the entire Arabian Peninsula. Only a cohesive political unit with a large population can stand up to a potential predator like Iran. In critical human mass lies the only way that the GCC can realistically guarantee its long-term survival.

About the Author

Ali is an analyst and commentator on Middle Eastern politics and economics with a particular focus on Saudi Arabia. After a career in banking based out of Riyadh and Dubai, Ali retired from finance to write. He is a graduate of Princeton University with a BA in politics and of the Harvard Business School with an MBA.

Website: www.alishihabi.com
Twitter: @alishihabi

Printed in the United States
By Bookmasters